Tempting Brooke

Also from Kristen Proby

The Big Sky Series:
Charming Hannah
Kissing Jenna
Waiting for Willa – Coming soon!

Kristen Proby's Crossover Collection – Coming March 12, 2019
Soaring With Fallon: A Big Sky Novel by Kristen Proby
Wicked Force: A Wicked Horse Vegas/Big Sky Novella
by Sawyer Bennett
All Stars Fall: A Seaside Pictures/Big Sky Novella
by Rachel Van Dyken
Hold On: A Play On/Big Sky Novella
by Samantha Young
Worth Fighting For: A Warrior Fight Club/Big Sky Novella
by Laura Kaye
Crazy Imperfect Love: A Dirty Dicks/Big Sky Novella
by K.L. Grayson
Nothing Without You: A Forever Yours/Big Sky Novella
by Monica Murphy

The Fusion Series:
Listen To Me
Close To You
Blush For Me
The Beauty of Us
Savor You

The Boudreaux Series:
Easy Love
Easy Charm
Easy Melody
Easy Kisses
Easy Magic
Easy Fortune
Easy Nights

Tempting Brooke

A Big Sky Novella

By Kristen Proby

1001 Dark Nights

EVIL EYE
CONCEPTS

Tempting Brooke
A Big Sky Novella
By Kristen Proby

1001 Dark Nights
Copyright 2018 Kristen Proby
ISBN: 978-1-948050-33-3

Foreword: Copyright 2014 M. J. Rose
Published by Evil Eye Concepts, Incorporated

Sign up for the 1001 Dark Nights Newsletter
and be entered to win a Tiffany Key necklace.

There's a contest every month!

Go to www.1001DarkNights.com to subscribe.

As a bonus, all subscribers will receive a free copy of
Discovery Bundle Three
Featuring stories by
Sidney Bristol, Darcy Burke, T. Gephart
Stacey Kennedy, Adriana Locke
JB Salsbury, and Erika Wilde

One Thousand and One Dark Nights

Once upon a time, in the future...

*I was a student fascinated with stories and learning.
I studied philosophy, poetry, history, the occult, and
the art and science of love and magic. I had a vast
library at my father's home and collected thousands
of volumes of fantastic tales.*

*I learned all about ancient races and bygone
times. About myths and legends and dreams of all
people through the millennium. And the more I read
the stronger my imagination grew until I discovered
that I was able to travel into the stories... to actually
become part of them.*

*I wish I could say that I listened to my teacher
and respected my gift, as I ought to have. If I had, I
would not be telling you this tale now.
But I was foolhardy and confused, showing off
with bravery.*

*One afternoon, curious about the myth of the
Arabian Nights, I traveled back to ancient Persia to
see for myself if it was true that every day Shahryar
(Persian: شهریار, "king") married a new virgin, and then
sent yesterday's wife to be beheaded. It was written
and I had read, that by the time he met Scheherazade,
the vizier's daughter, he'd killed one thousand
women.*

Something went wrong with my efforts. I arrived in the midst of the story and somehow exchanged places with Scheherazade — a phenomena that had never occurred before and that still to this day, I cannot explain.

Now I am trapped in that ancient past. I have taken on Scheherazade's life and the only way I can protect myself and stay alive is to do what she did to protect herself and stay alive.

Every night the King calls for me and listens as I spin tales. And when the evening ends and dawn breaks, I stop at a point that leaves him breathless and yearning for more. And so the King spares my life for one more day, so that he might hear the rest of my dark tale.

As soon as I finish a story... I begin a new one... like the one that you, dear reader, have before you now.

Prologue

~Brody~

My dad is an asshole. He's yelled and thrown fits my whole life. Whether he tried to scare me, or was just being a massive jerk, doesn't matter.

He's a dick.

But last night, he hit me for the first time. Like, full-out hit me because he said I'm a man now, and I can take it.

And I fucking hate him.

I'm meeting Brooke Henderson, my neighbor, at the end of our block, just like we always do on weekdays. We walk to school together every day, and have since we were in grade school.

She's been my friend forever. She's small, with long dark hair and big brown eyes, and she might be the one person in this world that I'd do almost anything for.

"Hey," she says with a big smile as I wait for her on the sidewalk. Her smile is my favorite. It reaches all the way to her eyes and lights up her whole face. "I'm *not* ready for Mr. Koch's math test today. I'm just so *bad* at it." She loops her arm through mine and offers me a bite of her breakfast burrito, which I happily accept. "Do you have any finals today?"

"Just English." I pass her burrito back and cringe when we walk down a curb. It makes my ribs sing in agony.

"Are you okay?" she asks, staring up at me with worried brown eyes, and I want to tell her everything. How he screams at both my mom and me for hours. How he used to smack her around, but now he's decided to move on to me.

But I can't because I'm afraid she'll never look at me the same way again, and I couldn't stand that.

"I'm fine," I lie. "Just didn't sleep a lot."

"I sleep like the dead," she says. "I slept until noon on Sunday. Noon! That can't be normal."

"It's probably normal." I don't think I've ever slept until noon. My dad would never permit it.

"We have to hurry." She picks up the pace, and I want to moan as my ribs cry out from keeping up with her. "I want to get to class early to get some math help."

"You know I'll help you whenever you want."

"Well, come on. I'll take you up on it."

* * * *

Three years, and I'm done.

That motherfucker put his hands on me for the last time yesterday. Just before graduation, he pulled me into his bedroom and kicked me in the ribs until I was sure I'd cough up blood. Trying to defend myself only makes it much worse.

As usual, my mom cried, and begged for him to stop, but it didn't do any good.

I'm eighteen. I have a car, and about a thousand dollars that I hid away over the past two years from my job. I begged Mom to go with me, to leave him and this good-for-nothing town and make a new start.

She refused.

I don't want to leave her, but if I stay, I'll end up killing him, and I don't want to spend the rest of my life in jail. I don't want to live like this anymore.

I need to leave.

This town never did anything good for me. Aside from Brooke, who I don't even speak to anymore because my life went into the shitter, and I didn't have the balls to talk to her about it.

Nothing good has come from being in Cunningham Falls.

I throw my one bag of clothes and personal things behind the seat of my Ford truck and speed off, not looking back.

Chapter One

~Brooke~

"I stopped at the post office and got the mail," my sister, Maisey, announces as she marches into my shop and drops a stack of envelopes and catalogues on my table.

"Thanks." I reach for the envelopes first and thumb through them. "Lots of bills here."

"Always," she says with a smirk. "Who knew that being a business owner would be so expensive?"

I stare at her for a moment and then bust out laughing. "*We* did."

"Oh yeah." She sniffs at some pink hydrangea blooms, fussing over them. Maisey and I are less than a year apart, so we've always been close. Opening businesses at the same time, and supporting each other through that process, just seemed natural.

An off-white envelope catches my eye, and I pull it out from the rest, immediately opening it.

"Holy shit," I mutter.

"What?"

"Hold on." I skim the letter, and then shake my head. "No. Absolutely not."

"What the hell?" Maisey demands, so I read the letter aloud.

Dear Ms. Henderson,

I've recently inherited the building your business resides in. I intend to sell the building. This is your sixty-day notice to vacate. I'll be in Cunningham Falls next week to meet with you in person, should it be necessary.

Respectfully,
Brody Chabot

"Shit," Maisey whispers and drags her fingers down her face. "I guess that means I can't rent the space next door now."

Maisey makes delicious wedding cakes, and her business has skyrocketed in the past year. She's been baking out of her house, and we host tastings here in my shop. When the space next door became vacant, she was hoping to move her bakery in there.

We both were.

"This isn't going to happen," I insist and fold the letter, place it back in its envelope, and move on to the next thing.

"With all due respect, how in the hell do you propose to stop it? It's not like we can afford to buy the building. In downtown Cunningham Falls, this would go for several million dollars."

"I'm going to talk him out of it."

She stares at me, then shakes her head and lets out a laugh. "Okay, I gotta hear this. How, exactly, do you intend to do that? I know that you and Brody were close when we were kids, but you haven't seen him in more than ten years. Are you going to hypnotize him or something?"

"No, I'm going to have a calm, adult conversation with him."

"This is business, big sister." She reaches over to smack a kiss on my cheek. "For purely selfish reasons, I hope you make it happen. I'm sick of baking at my house. I don't have enough counter space. But Brody got out of here as soon as he could, and I suspect that this building isn't something he wants to keep."

"Well, he's going to," I reply, sounding way more confident than I feel. "Businesses, especially new businesses, don't do well when they have to relocate. We're doing *so great*, Maisey. And with you next door, well, there's so much more we could do."

"I don't disagree with you," she says. "This is an ideal location, and we *are* doing great. I'd like to be a fly on the wall when you talk to Brody. He was hot back in the day."

I don't respond, but my stomach does a little flop. He was *so hot*. And so freaking nice. And then one day, he stopped walking me to school. No explanation. Nothing. He just wasn't my friend anymore.

I've wondered for years what I did wrong. Brody was someone that I truly cared about and enjoyed spending time with. And to say that I had a crush on him is the understatement of the year.

He was hot, kind, and smiled at me unlike anyone else ever has, before or since.

I hope there's a piece of that boy still in there, and that when I talk to him, I can make him see reason. Because I'm not moving Brooke's Blooms out of this building.

* * * *

"Stop pacing," Maisey says the following week. I'm walking back and forth through the flower shop, biting my thumbnail and stressing the hell out.

"Why is she acting like this?" Micah, my teenage afternoon help, asks Maisey. Micah is seventeen, and comes in after school to process deliveries, trim stems, and clean up. He's tall and lanky with dark hair that falls into his eyes. Sometimes a bit clumsy. And we adore him.

"She's seeing a guy she hasn't seen in a long time."

"Like, on a date?"

"No." I turn, my hands on my hips, and pin them both with a glare. "It's not a date. It's a business meeting. Because I'm a business woman."

"Adults are weird," he mumbles as he carries an armload of roses into the cooler, just when the bell on the front door dings, and there he is in the flesh.

Brody Chabot.

"Brooke?" A slow grin spreads over that sexy mouth, and I have to take a minute to just soak him in. He's grown a couple more inches, making him ridiculously tall. His dark hair is cut short around his ears, and a little longer on top, stylishly messy.

He's in cargo shorts and a polo shirt, due to it being the hottest day of the year so far out there.

"Hi, Brody," I reply and swallow hard. "Thanks for meeting with me."

"Hi, Brody," Maisey says with a smile. "Welcome back."

He blinks and nods, then tosses her a friendly smile. "Thanks. Good to see you." He turns back to me as he tucks his sunglasses in his pocket. "I thought, since the space next door is empty, we could walk over there."

I nod and tuck a piece of my hair behind my ear. "That works. Maisey, do you and Micah have this?"

"Of course. Take your time."

I send her a look that says *thanks, but if I'm not back in an hour, come get me.*

Brody leads the way and unlocks the glass door, then holds it open for me and waits for me to go ahead of him. He locks the door back up and follows me in.

The room is empty, aside from a glass countertop that used to display knick knacks. Brody walks behind it and leans on it casually, crosses his arms over his chest, and takes a moment to look me up and down, from my toes to my head.

"You still look sixteen," he says quietly. Just like that, his voice does things to me. It's deeper now, and his brown eyes aren't the eyes of a boy anymore. He's 100% pure sexy man, and I'm suddenly wishing I'd asked Maisey to attend this meeting with me.

"I don't feel sixteen," I reply with a small laugh and rest my hands on the countertop across from him. I'm only five-feet-two, so I have to look way up to meet his gaze. His eyes are guarded, but happy. I look at his left hand, and notice that he isn't wearing a ring.

"You're not wearing one either," he says quietly.

"No."

He nods once. "I'm assuming you wanted to meet about the letter."

"I do, yes. Brody, I need you to reconsider."

His eyebrows climb in surprise. "Excuse me?"

"You heard me. I'd like you to reconsider selling the building. If you sell, and I have to relocate, I could very well go out of business, and this business is important, Brody."

"To you."

"To this community."

He sneers, and I feel a bit of resentment bubble up in my gut. "I know you don't think very highly of Cunningham Falls, but it's a great place, and my flower shop is important here."

He purses his lips, not replying for a moment. "I don't want to sound condescending, Brooke. You're a smart woman, and I can see that your shop is nice. But it's flowers. It's not a doctor's office. Not to mention, I'm not asking you to close your business. You can relocate."

I want to bristle and toss back something rude, but this is Brody, and I know he doesn't mean to hurt my feelings.

"That's just it, I *can't* relocate. Location is *everything*, Brody. I've built a reputation in this place, and my customers already know where to find me. Also, commercial rental space is impossible to find in downtown. Businesses stay, and they don't close down because they do well.

"Brody, if you sell this building, someone will tear it down and build expensive condos here in its place. This *can't* happen."

"I think you're being melodramatic," he replies. "I'm sure the new owner, whomever it may be, will continue to rent to you."

"I know you don't understand," I say softly. "Let's table this discussion for just a minute. Can I ask you a question?"

"Sure." He narrows his eyes and seems to steel himself, getting ready.

"Where did you go? When you left?"

He sighs. "San Francisco."

"Oh." I pace away and then turn to look at him. "I missed you. I've thought of you often over the past ten years."

"I know I should have said goodbye, but—"

"Yes. You should have." I nod and wander back to him. "I worried for a while because I didn't see you, even around town. And then I heard someone say that you'd moved away."

"I'm sorry if I hurt your feelings."

"You did that long before you left," I reply and watch as he frowns and looks down at the counter. "But that's not what this is about. I was just curious as to where you went. I know that you couldn't get out of here fast enough, and I don't know why. But I can tell you that this community isn't as bad as you think it is."

He smirks, but there's no humor there. "We had different experiences."

"Let me show you." His gaze whips up to mine in surprise. "Let me prove to you that not only is owning this building a great investment, but that mine and Maisey's businesses are important to this community."

"How do you propose to do that? Show me your ledgers?"

"No, I'm going to do better than that. How long are you staying?"

"I'm leaving as soon as possible."

I frown, not sure why that hurts my heart as badly as it does. Standing here, talking to him like this, feels so good. I don't want him to leave.

"Can you give me a week?" Why didn't I think of this sooner? This is brilliant!

"A week?"

I nod, and watch as the wheels in his head start to spin. "I want one week. You can hang out in the shop as much or as little as you want, my only request is that you help build and deliver one order a day for the next week. An order that I choose."

"Look, Brooke, I appreciate that you have a business to run, but so do I. This is just business. It isn't personal."

"Not to me it isn't just business, and if you agree to do this, you'll see why."

He shakes his head and pushes his hand through his hair, the same way he used to when he was young and frustrated with me, which wasn't often.

But it's even sexier now.

"I don't really have time to stay for the week."

I cock my head to the side, watching him.

"What do you do in San Francisco?"

"I'm an engineer. I build bridges."

I feel my eyes widen, and I hold my hand up for a high-five. He laughs and obliges, and I can't help but notice how warm his palm is against mine.

"Good for you, Brody. That's awesome. I'd like to hear more about it. Over the next week."

He laughs now and paces away from me, then back.

"You're as stubborn now as you were at fifteen."

"No, I'm much more stubborn now."

He shakes his head, watching me with hot eyes. This isn't the way a teenager would look at me.

This is a man.

And holy crap, he's potent, and hotter than ever.

But he's also a stranger now, and the owner of my building. I need to keep it that way.

"Do it for me," I say, batting my eyelashes. I smile as he breaks out into a laugh.

"I never could tell you no. But, Brooke, just because I'm going to do this with you doesn't mean that I'm not selling this building."

"I know." *You're not selling. I'll talk you out of it.* "Can you start tomorrow?"

"The sooner the better. I have some calls to make."

He walks me out and we stop in front of the shop. "You won't regret this," I say and pat his bicep, then blink rapidly at the rock-hard muscles I come in contact with. Jesus, he's just… *hard.*

"Oh, I think that's probably the biggest lie you've ever told." He winks and walks down the street. I can't take my eyes off his backside. His broad shoulders.

We both might live to regret it.

Chapter Two

~Brody~

Well, that didn't go as planned.

I was supposed to be in Cunningham Falls for a grand total of fourteen hours before I got back on a plane to San Francisco, leaving Montana in the rear-view for good.

Instead, I just agreed to spend a week delivering flowers.

Am I out of my fucking mind?

I shake my head as I walk down the sidewalk, past restaurants and shops, toward my car. It took me forever to find a place to park today. I guess Cunningham Falls isn't quite as sleepy as it was when I was young.

Yes, it would seem I *am* out of my mind. At least, when I'm around Brooke. I never could tell her no, and it looks like that hasn't changed at all.

Brooke is a different story. I wasn't lying when I said she hasn't aged a bit. Her face is still fresh and sweet, that mole above her lip making my heart thump in my chest and my dick twitch in ways it never did when I was fifteen.

But the rest of her? Jesus H. Christ, she's become a sexy woman. She's curvier, and carries those curves well on her small frame. I wanted to boost her up on that counter top, wrap her stiletto-tipped legs around my hips, and get acquainted with her in a whole new way.

And I'm pretty sure that makes me an asshole.

"Brody? Brody Chabot?"

I stop, scowl, and turn, shocked as fuck that someone would

recognize me. But the scowl falls away when I see Mrs. Blakely sweeping the sidewalk in front of *Little Deli*, the restaurant she's owned on Main Street since before I can remember.

"Mrs. Blakely." I lean in to kiss her cheek and she pats my arm, similar to the way Brooke did, but my body's response is completely different this time. "How are you?"

"Well, I'm fantastic now. Don't tell me you're going to walk past my place and not come in for a pastrami sandwich."

"I wouldn't dare," I reply, even though I'm not hungry, and I need to find a hotel and a place to get to work, clearing my schedule for the week.

"Good." She leans her broom outside the door and leads me inside. It's past lunch time, so it's quiet in her deli right now, and she points to the stool I used to occupy every afternoon after school. "Your seat's open."

"I see that." I straddle the stool and lean my elbows on the counter, watching Mrs. Blakely bustle around, making me my favorite sandwich. "How are you, ma'am?"

"Never better," she says with a grin. "Happy to see you, and that's the truth of it. I should twist your ear off for being gone so long without coming to visit me."

"It's been a long time," I agree as she puts the finishing touches on my sandwich and passes it over to me. I take a big bite, and I'm immediately seventeen again, talking with Mrs. Blakely, eating my afternoon sandwich that she never charged me for, and it doesn't feel as bad as I thought it would.

"Good?"

"Oh my God," I groan and take another bite. "I didn't think I was hungry."

Her face lights up in happiness as she puts everything away and wipes down her workspace.

"Now, what have you been up to, Brody?"

"Living in San Francisco, working mostly."

"Wife? Kids?"

I shake my head no. I almost got married once, but we both came to our senses about six months before the wedding and realized that we weren't meant to be together forever.

"Neither. How are all of your children?"

She smiles again and gives me the rundown on where all four of her kids are, who's married, and who's not.

"My Stephanie isn't married," she says. "And she lives in L.A."

"No, thanks." I hold my hands up and laugh around my last bite of sandwich. "I'm not on the market."

"Let me know if you change your mind," she says with a wink. "What are you in town for?"

"Glen passed away," I reply.

"Yes, I was at your father's funeral," she says. What she doesn't say is *you weren't.*

"I inherited some property and personal things, and I just came to town to take care of that."

Her eyes are shrewd, and I expect questions. She asked a lot of questions when I was a kid and spent too many hours perched on this stool.

But she doesn't ask. She just nods and then takes my empty plate away.

"Well, I'm glad I got to see you while you were here," she says. "And I sure was sorry about your dad. He was such a good man."

Bull. Fucking. Shit. No one knew what kind of man my father really was because neither I or my mom ever told them.

Glen Chabot played the part well for the rest of the community. Devoted husband and father. Shrewd businessman. Member of the city council.

Cunningham Falls fucking loved him. I bet there was a parade in his honor after the bastard died.

But no one ever knew who he really was. No one but me and my mom, who passed away from breast cancer several years ago. I offered to come back for her, but she refused. She was determined that I remember her as being healthy, but she was wrong. I'll always remember her as beaten, and not from the cancer.

Rather than say all of that to Mrs. Blakely, I just offer her a smile and say, "Thank you."

The bell above the door dings as a customer walks in, and my smile dies on my lips when I see who it is.

Grayson King was the only other friend that I had in town, and I didn't say goodbye to him, either.

But rather than cuss me out, he smiles widely and holds his hand out to shake mine, pulling me in for a hug.

"Brody, shit, I didn't know you were in town."

"I was supposed to be in and out, but it looks like I'll be here for a week or so."

He sits on the stool next to mine and says hello to Mrs. Blakely, then orders a turkey sandwich. "Give me your number, and Noah and I'll take you out for a beer."

Noah is his older brother, and we used to play together as kids. I've wondered about both of them over the years.

"I'll take you up on that," I reply and pull my phone out. I've missed a text from Brooke.

Meet me at the shop at 10:00, please.

I quickly reply before taking Gray's number and shooting him a text.

I've been in town for three hours, and I'm already deeply entrenched in the past, something I was trying to avoid.

But it doesn't feel nearly as horrible as I thought it would.

* * * *

"We cut the stems like this," Brooke says the next morning. We're standing at her work table, gloves on, and there is a mountain of fresh flowers before us, waiting to be clipped, sorted, and put away. She snips the end, peels off a bunch of the leaves, tossing them in the compost basket, and then puts the flower in a bucket of fresh water. "Then, Micah will carry the flowers into the cooler when he arrives in a couple of hours. We should have all of this done by the time he gets here."

"This is a shit ton of flowers," I say, surveying it all.

"This will get me through a couple of days," she says proudly and reaches for a rose. "Don't cut them down too much because we'll clip them once more when they go in their arrangements."

I follow her direction, and when she's satisfied that I'm doing it correctly, she moves on to other things.

The bell over the door, exactly the same as Mrs. Blakely's, dings and a man walks in, approaching Brooke.

"Hello, Mr. King," she says, catching my attention. I poke my head out from behind the flowers and smile when I see Jeffrey King,

Gray's uncle. "I already have your usual bouquet ready."

"You're a sweetheart," he says, then sees me and his face lights up. "Well, Brody! It's good to see you."

"You too, sir."

Jeffrey King and his two sons own and operate a large ranch outside of Cunningham Falls. His boys were a few years older than me and their cousins, but we would go out to the ranch a couple of times each summer to ride horses and run wild.

I'd forgotten about those days.

"How is the ranch?" I ask.

"Oh, it's doing just fine. Zack and Josh run it now, and their mother and I have retired."

"Good for you."

Brooke walks out of the cooler, holding a huge bouquet of yellow roses.

"Ah, there they are," Jeffrey says and takes them from her. "You'll put this on my tab, right?"

"Of course," she says with a wide smile.

"My pretty bride will love them." He winks at both of us. "Good to see you, Brody. Oh, and I'm sorry about your dad."

"Have a great day," I reply with a wave as he walks out of the shop. "Does he come in often?"

"Every week, same time," Brooke replies. "Always buys his wife yellow roses. He's done it since the week I opened."

"That's sweet," I say and can't resist reaching over to smooth a piece of her dark chestnut hair off her cheek. "I always liked the King family."

"Me too," she says and moves away from me, but not before I see the heat rise in her face. It seems I'm not the only one attracted. "They're growing like crazy, too. Josh and Zack both have kids now."

"Didn't Zack go into the Army?"

"He did, but he's been home for a few years now. He married Jillian Sullivan, and they have twins, with another baby on the way. Zack also has a teenage son, from a previous marriage."

"That's a lot of kids," I reply with a laugh.

"Hey, I just want to say, I'm sorry about your dad, too. He was always really nice to me."

I take a deep breath, the aroma of the flowers filling my head, and try to push out the hatred I still carry for Glen. I can't say thank you, not to Brooke. It's fake, and I've never been fake with her. That's why I couldn't be her friend anymore in high school.

She would have figured out my horrible home life because I never could lie to her.

"Don't be," I reply softly, watching the stems as I clip them.

"What?" She steps closer to me and rubs her hand up and down my arm. Being in direct physical contact with Brooke isn't a good idea.

All I've been able to think about since I left her yesterday was getting in her pants.

She absolutely shouldn't touch me.

"What do you mean?" she asks again.

"Nothing." I shove a final stem in a bucket, filling it. "I can carry this in the cooler. No need to wait for Micah." I lift it and walk away, hoping she'll drop the subject.

I'm not disappointed when I walk out. Maisey's arrived, carrying cake samples.

"We have a wedding cake and flower appointment this evening," Maisey says with a smile. "But I brought extras for you."

"Well, you're officially my new favorite person," I reply and pull her in for a hug. Maisey is just as beautiful as her sister. Smart. Funny.

But my body has zero reaction when I touch her. It's what case studies are made of, but I'll never tell anyone.

Especially Brooke.

"Here, try the chocolate with strawberry frosting first."

Maisey passes me the plate and I bite in, then look up in absolute shock. "Holy fuck."

"Good, right?" Maisey asks with a smug smile.

"How do you not weigh seven thousand pounds? I'd never stop eating this."

She laughs and shakes her head. "I taste it here and there, to make sure it's perfect. Here, I have huckleberry."

"I haven't had huckleberry anything since I was a kid." I take the cake and try to hide how damn good it is, but it's no use. I moan and lean against the counter as if I'm dying. "Jesus, Maisey. You're absolutely doing what you're meant to do."

"Thanks." She takes the rest in the cooler for later, then comes back out.

"She'd like to rent the empty space next door," Brooke adds, giving me a sweet smile. "We'd like to expand a bit, offer more high-end gifts, and be able to host bouquet building parties, or cake decorating parties. The possibilities are endless."

Except I'm selling the building.

"I could definitely use the extra counter space," Maisey adds with a vigorous nod. "I'm so sick of working in my kitchen at home."

"You don't have an industrial space?"

She shakes her head no. "That's why I come here to offer cake tastings to potential brides. Plus, we can combine the appointments. I give them cake options, and Brooke can go over flowers with them, too."

"It works well, and I think we could expand it even more if she were right next door."

I take a final bite of cake, watching the two beautiful women as they tell me their plans, knowing full well that I've just been ambushed.

"You did this on purpose."

Brooke blinks her big brown eyes. "Whatever do you mean?"

"You brought in this delicious cake, and just pitched me your business ideas, hoping to sway me from selling the building."

"Well, we aren't stupid, Brody," Maisey says with a shrug. "You're a captive audience. Of course we did."

I laugh and toss my fork and paper plate in the garbage, then reach for a napkin to wipe my mouth.

"Pretty smart," I agree. "Maybe whomever I sell the building to will lease it back to you."

They look at each other and then shake their heads in defeat.

"I told you—"

"I know," Brooke says, interrupting me. "You're selling. Doesn't mean I won't keep trying, Brody."

She offers me a sad smile, and then walks into the cooler, then back out with a huge bouquet.

"It's time to deliver these," she says and reaches for her keys and purse. "Come on."

Chapter Three

~Brooke~

"Isn't this the Cunningham place?" Brody asks twenty minutes later as we approach one of the biggest and oldest homes in town.

"Yep," I reply with a smile that I really don't feel. Despite Maisey's delicious cake today, and our brilliant business plan, we didn't seem to sway Brody on his decision to sell the building.

I know it's only day one, but I can't help but feel some disappointment.

"Lauren Cunningham, now Sullivan, lives here with her husband and their kids."

"Ty Sullivan?" he asks.

"That's the one," I reply and feel the usual excitement I get when I know I'm going to see Ty. Don't get me wrong, he's married, and I'm no home wrecker, but I've had a tiny crush on the bad boy lawyer since I was a kid. I think most women in town do. He's just... *crushable*. I climb out of my SUV and walk to the back where the flowers are secured. I reach for them, but Brody stops me.

"I'll get them."

"They aren't heavy."

"You have me here to work," he reminds me. "So I'm working."

"Touché." I laugh and lead him up the steps to the front door and ring the bell. A few moments later, Ty appears, looking completely disheveled, his dark hair a riot, his face covered in stubble, and rather than his usual suit, he's in jeans and a Metallica T-shirt.

With baby puke on the front.

"Hey, Brooke," he says with a half smile. "Let's keep our voices down, okay? I just got Layla down for a nap. She insists she's too old, but with the new baby and all the chaos, she needed it."

"We won't be long," I reply with a hushed voice. "I have these flowers for Lo, and I admit, I'd love to see the new little one."

"Of course," Ty says, his tired face transforming into the brightest smile in Montana. "They're in the office. This way."

He leads us into Lo's office, where she's sitting in her chaise lounge, smiling softly as she watches the little baby sleep in a bassinet next to her.

"Brooke," she says with a smile and stands to give me a hug. "How are you?"

"I'm great. You look fantastic for just having had a baby two days ago."

She glances at Ty, and then back at the baby. "I feel good. I was going to get some writing in, but I can't stop staring at him."

"Lo, do you remember Brody?"

She looks at Brody and grins. "Of course. Wow, I almost didn't recognize you. Are you working for Brooke now?"

"Sort of," he says as he passes the flowers to Ty, who puts them on Lo's desk and pulls the card out of the arrangement for her before shaking Brody's hand. "I'm helping her out this week."

"Fun," Lo says and sits down again, cringing a bit as she pulls her legs up and takes the card from Ty. "Aww, you got me *more* flowers?"

"I'm buying you flowers every day," he says as he leans in to kiss her. "You earned them."

"You're sweet," Lo says with a grin and turns to me. "Do you want to hold him?"

"I didn't want to ask, but man, do I," I reply with a chuckle. "Do you mind?"

"Not at all."

I reach in for the sleeping baby, and cradle him to me, kissing his soft head. "Oh, he has auburn hair like his mama."

"Seems both of my kids will be gingers," Ty says with a happy smile. "They'll keep me on my toes."

"Oh, Lo, he's so beautiful. What did you name him?"

"We haven't announced it yet, but if you can keep a secret, we'll tell you," Lo says.

I'm rocking the baby back and forth. I can't take my eyes off his sweet face. His perfect lips are making little sucking motions as he dreams.

"I'm not going to tell anyone," I reply and kiss his soft forehead again.

"Logan Jeffrey," Ty replies as he rubs circles over his wife's back. "For Jeffrey King."

"Oh, that's so sweet," I reply and kiss little Logan's cheek one more time before giving him back to his mama. "I know that you're close to Zack and Josh."

"Jeffrey practically raised me," Ty replies. "He's the only dad I know. He definitely saved me from the man who fathered me."

Brody tenses beside me, and I glace up at him, but his face hasn't changed a bit. Did I imagine it?

"Congratulations," Brody says and smiles down at the baby. "He's a sweet little guy."

"Thank you," Lo says. "I'm so happy that you both stopped by. Have you moved back to town, Brody?"

He shakes his head and shoves his hands in his pockets. "No. I'm just here for the week."

"Well, enjoy your time here," Ty says as he leads us back to the front door. When Lo's out of ear shot, he grins down at me. "And thanks for those. They're exactly what I wanted, just like the flowers along the fenceline."

"And down her back," I add with a grin. "I have tattoo envy."

His smile grows. "You did great. I'll see you soon."

We hurry down to the car and climb inside, and pull away from the massive home, my windshield wipers moving swiftly in the sudden summer rain.

"So, the man looks amazing in a suit *and* in baby puke. Who knew?"

"What?" Brody's head whips around, and he's staring at me like I just said I'm an alien.

"I've had a crush on Ty for *years*. I love me a man in a sexy suit. I had no idea that he looked good in a rocker T-shirt, too."

"He's married," he replies with a frown.

"Oh, please. I'm no home wrecker. But a girl can look. Especially when he fills out a suit the way that Ty does. Not to mention, he *loves* his wife. You should see some of the flower arrangements he's had me make for her. He's a total romantic."

"I wear suits," Brody says, rather defensively.

"You do?"

"Every damn day."

"Hmm." I glance his way and then back to the road. "I don't buy it. Prove it."

He laughs next to me, then pulls his phone out, taps it, and holds it up for me to see. There he is, on the screen, wearing a suit.

"That could have been for one occasion."

But my God, he looks *delicious* in that photo. I wonder if there's a way that I could get it from him, to have after he leaves.

"That's how I look every day."

"Not today."

He's quiet, so I look his way and giggle at the look of absolute frustration on his handsome face.

"I'm not wearing a suit to the flower shop."

"Well, how are you going to prove it, then?"

He tucks his phone in his pocket and rubs his hand over his face, then shakes his head and laughs. "I suppose I'll have to take you out to dinner."

My gaze whips to his in surprise. "Really?"

"Yeah. Dinner."

"When?"

"Tonight," he says and reaches over to brush a knuckle down my cheek. "Are you free?"

I swallow hard as I park the car. "Yeah. I'm free."

"I'll pick you up at seven."

* * * *

Dinner wasn't in my plans. I'm beginning to think it's a bad idea to have Brody come to the flower shop every day as it is because whenever I'm within ten feet of him, I want to lick him.

I'm pretty sure that would be considered sexual harassment in the workplace, even though he's not on my payroll.

I stare at myself in the mirror as I brush the curls I just put in my long, dark hair and then laugh at myself.

Brody is just being nice. I practically pushed him into a corner this afternoon, and he asked me to dinner. He's my friend, and that's it.

I brush some gloss on my lips, and take stock. Flowy red summer dress: check. Natural makeup: check. Butterflies: check.

The bell dings, and I reach for my small handbag and answer the door.

Brody's eyes start at my face and slowly meander down my body to my sandal-covered feet, and if I'm not mistaken, his jaw clenches.

Just friends, Brooke.

"Hey."

I can't help but take my own perusal of the man standing before me. Jesus in a basket, he fills out a suit nicely. His shoulders are broad, and his arms muscular.

Yes, this does things to me.

"Can I come in?" he asks with a small smile on his lips.

"Of course." I step back and he walks inside my small house.

"This is nice," he says, but his eyes are still on me.

"Thanks. I've been here for a couple of years." I glance around, wondering if Brody and I have the same tastes, and then I glance back to him and bust out laughing.

"What?" he asks.

"Turn around." He complies, and I reach up to pull the tag that's poked out of the neck of his jacket. His hair is soft against the back of my fingers, and I can't help but wonder what it would feel like as I fist it while he does amazing, sexy things to me.

I take a deep breath and hand it to him with a laugh. "Wear it every day, my ass."

He tucks the tag in his pocket. "I didn't bring a suit to Montana. I had to improvise."

He bought it just for me.

And according to the tag, it wasn't cheap.

Now I feel bad. I shouldn't have pushed the issue. He spent a bunch of money that he didn't need to, all because I gave him a hard time.

"I thought we could eat at *Ciao* tonight," he says as he leads me out of the house to his rented convertible. The sun broke out a couple of hours ago, and it's the perfect temperature now. But I just did my hair.

I think about asking him to put the top up, and then decide, *fuck it.*

I reach into my handbag and pull out a hair tie, twist my hair on top of my head, and grin as I sit in the fun car.

"I could have put the top up."

"And that would have been a waste on a day like today," I reply smoothly and have to physically restrain myself from reaching over to brush my fingertips through that soft hair at the nape of his neck.

We drive through town in silence. Rather than park in front of the restaurant, he drives past, and I frown over at him.

"Having second thoughts?"

"No." He sends me a smile. "Before we go in, I'd like to know why you got so quiet."

I bite my lip and look out my window, then turn to him and say, "Did you buy that suit just for me?"

"Seems I do a lot of things for you lately," he replies with a grin. "It's not a big deal, Brooke."

"I'm sorry," I reply. "I was just goofing around this afternoon. I didn't mean for you to have to do all of this."

"All of what?"

"Buy that gorgeous suit, take me to dinner. I feel like I hijacked your day, and I feel bad."

He pulls over, whips his seatbelt off, and turns to me.

"Look at me."

I comply. He drags his knuckle down my cheek again, and that's all it takes to set my body on high alert.

I don't think my nipples will ever be anything but hard again.

"You've hijacked my whole week," he reminds me, making me giggle. I cover my mouth with my hand. "And I invited you to dinner because I wanted to. I enjoy spending time with you, Brooke. I always have."

"Is your girlfriend pissed that you're in Montana?" I ask, not even trying to hide that I'm digging for information.

"Yes," he says and I feel my eyes go wide in mortification. He laughs, hard, like he used to when we were teens. "Jesus, the look on your face is priceless."

"Tell me you *don't* have a girlfriend."

"Why?"

"Because if you do, the thoughts running through my head will surely put me straight into hell."

His eyes narrow on me and he leans in close, just a few inches from me. "What thoughts are those?"

"I'm not telling."

His brown eyes fall to my lips, then move back to my own. "I'll get some wine in you. You'll talk."

I snort as he pulls back out onto the street, circles back to the restaurant, and easily finds a spot, which is hard to do this time of year.

He shocks the hell out of me by taking my hand in his, linking our fingers as we walk inside. His hand is warm, but not sweaty. Dry and smooth, but not cracked or callused.

Frankly, it feels fantastic.

"Two, please," he tells the hostess. He never lets go of my hand as we're led through the dining room to a table by the front windows, in the corner. When our hands pull away so we can sit, I feel a loss that seems absolutely ridiculous. "Is the food good here?" he asks after the hostess leaves.

"Mm. Oh, that's right, this didn't open until after you left."

"The hotel recommended it," he says with a nod. "It smells good."

"Wait until you taste the bread. You'll never be the same."

He grins at me, and my heart stops. I've known this man forever, and yet, I *don't* know him. I recognize his face, but I don't recognize the firm body that's come with being a man.

And I have absolutely no idea what his life has consisted of over the past ten-plus years.

"Tell me everything," I blurt out.

"About what?"

"About everything. I don't know anything about you anymore, and that makes me a little sad."

He sighs and reaches over to squeeze my hand. He doesn't let go.

"I don't know anything about you, either." He frowns, looking at our fingers, seemingly lost in his own thoughts. "But we have a week to learn."

"Let's start now," I suggest, making him laugh.

"Well, one thing I know is that you're still as impatient as you ever were."

I nod, but we're interrupted by the waitress, who goes through her whole spiel of wine and specials. She writes her name on the paper on our table. Once she's taken our order and leaves, Brody says, "So, what's your verdict on the suit?"

I let my eyes travel over him, taking in the navy suit and white button-down under it. He's paired it with a lighter blue tie that sets off his brown eyes.

I'm pretty sure my panties are soaked.

"It's good."

His eyes narrow. "It's just *good?*"

I shrug, take a sip of my water, and look away. No, it's not just *good*. It's fucking brilliant. I want to rip it off of him to see what's beneath it.

But that seems a bit forward.

"I mean, if you like that sort of thing."

He sits back in his chair, staring at me. "You confessed this afternoon that you do like that sort of thing."

I smile, holding his gaze as the waitress delivers our drinks and leaves. Neither of us takes a sip.

"You look damn good in that suit, Brody."

He smiles now, a bit shyly, and then he looks me over, the way he did when I first opened the door to him.

"You're just... wow." I cock a brow, and he slowly shakes his head.

"You were always a beautiful girl, Brooke. But damn, you're stunning. Thanks for coming to dinner with me."

"Thanks for inviting me."

The time flies by as we dig into our food, and Brody falls head over heels in love with the garlic bread.

I told him he would.

We're both fat and happy as we mosey out of the restaurant, toward his car.

"God, I can barely move," I moan as I drop into the seat and rub my food baby. "Why do I always eat too much?"

"Because it's delicious," he says and sighs when he sits next to me. "All of my clothes are suddenly too small."

I laugh and nod. "Me, too."

He drives us back to my house, parks at the curb, and is still the perfect gentleman as he opens my door and escorts me to my porch.

"Do you want to come inside?" I ask as I unlock the door.

"Yes," he says with a sigh, leaning his shoulder on the frame and looking down at me with longing. "So I'd better go."

I nod and paste a smile on my face, determined to not let him see my disappointment. I'd like to spend more time with him. It's easy, just like it was before, with a new sexual tension that's just exhilarating.

"Well, you have a good night. Thanks for dinner."

I turn to go inside, but he stops me, framing my face with his big hands.

Is he going to kiss me? Please, God, kiss me. I bet he'd win an Olympic gold medal if it were a sport.

He leans in, his eyes on my lips, and I brace myself for the kiss of the century.

But he plants his lips on my forehead, takes a deep breath, and then pulls away.

"See you tomorrow, Brooke."

He walks away and I hurry inside, shut the door, and lean my back against it. My heart is hammering in my chest, my breath coming as fast as if I'd just run a marathon.

Not that I know what that feels like, since I only run if something's chasing me.

I'm an idiot. I've been on fire all evening, enjoying his touches and our conversation, and I wanted nothing more than for him to kiss me.

And he was just being nice.

Because he's my friend.

And that's all he's ever going to be.

Chapter Four

~Brody~

I'm a fucking idiot.

I wanted to kiss her. Hell, I wanted to take her inside, strip her out of that dress, and explore every delectable inch of her tiny little body.

And if she wasn't giving off *kiss me* signals, I'll be damned to hell.

She's absolutely on the same page. But this is *Brooke*. The girl I used to care about when I was a kid, and let's not forget that I'm leaving in just a few days.

While I wouldn't mind a romp in bed with a willing, beautiful partner, it just can't be Brooke.

I'm not an asshole.

I pull into the hotel on the lake where I'm staying, hand my keys to the valet, and ride up the elevator to my room. I'm on the top floor, but at only four floors up, that's not saying too much.

Cunningham Falls has always had a height restriction on buildings, only allowing them to be four stories high, and no taller.

But I'm high enough up that I have a killer view of the lake and the ski mountain. I walk out onto the balcony and sit in the fancy outdoor couch, kick my feet up, and cross my hands over my still-full belly.

I've come a long way. I started out as an abused kid, living not even a mile from here. And now, I'm in the biggest room the hotel has, in a thousand-dollar suit that I had the concierge find for me this afternoon.

I didn't lie when I told Brooke that I'm an engineer.

I just didn't tell her that I own the firm. And I did it all without one single penny from Glen.

I sigh, drag my hands down my face, and then frown when my phone vibrates in my pocket.

"Chabot," I answer.

"Hey, boss," Van, my assistant, says. "How's Montana?"

"Hot," I reply and grin. I wouldn't be able to function without Van. He is way more than an assistant. He has excellent instincts, and he's trustworthy.

That's the most important part.

"I have a few things to go over," Van continues, and we spend the next thirty minutes talking about current projects that several of my engineers are working on. Once he's caught me up to speed, he takes a deep breath, and I know he's about to start asking personal questions.

This is Van, after all.

"So, *why* are you still in Montana? You were supposed to be back two days ago."

I sigh and watch as a bald eagle flies over the lake, then swoops down and plucks a fish out of the water. I'd forgotten how late it is when the sun goes down this far north.

"Good question," I murmur. I can't exactly tell him that I'm here because there's a certain brunette that's captured my attention. He'd call me seven different kinds of a moron, and he wouldn't be wrong.

I have a business, and a life, to get back to in California.

"My father's estate is taking longer than I thought to settle."

It's not a lie.

"When do you want me to arrange for you to come back?" he asks. "I'll book the tickets tonight."

"Next week," I reply and can almost hear his scowl from a thousand miles away. "I can work remotely."

"Do you need me to come there?"

"No. I'm fine. I'll work remotely, and you can continue to call me daily with updates. If you need anything, I always have my phone on me."

"Sounds good. Talk to you tomorrow, boss."

He hangs up and I drop my phone in my lap. I forgot that the pace here is much slower than in San Francisco. To say it's calmer is the understatement of the year. I don't remember the last time I sat outside just to watch an eagle fly.

Or at all, for that matter.

I usually fall asleep on the sofa of my office, then get up the next day and do it all again. I'm a workaholic, just like the asshole who raised me. The only good thing Glen Chabot ever gave me was his work ethic.

I've put it to good use.

And until two days ago, I would have said that it was enough for me. That I was perfectly content.

How could Brooke change things so quickly?

* * * *

"This is a huge arrangement for someone's table," I comment the next afternoon as Brooke shows me how to stick stems into this green foam stuff to make it stay in place and look nice.

"It's not going on a table. It's going on a casket." She smiles sadly and then walks to the other side of her work station to consult her notebook.

"Oh." I frown, pausing in placing the sunflower in the green foam. "Who died?"

"Derek Snyder," she says, then looks up at me with a sigh. "We need to make a similar bouquet to this one and deliver it to his widow today."

"Sunflowers? Don't most people get calla lilies or roses?"

"He preferred sunflowers," she says. "I met with him several times, and he was very specific about what he wanted."

"He planned his own funeral."

"Every detail." She nods, passes me another flower, and then gets to work helping me. "Let's finish this up so we can work on his wife's arrangement."

We spend a good hour working on the massive arrangement for his casket, and then Brooke reaches for a vase, another green foamy thing, and we built a similar bouquet to the one for the funeral.

"This is lovely," she says, turning the finished product around in a circle, checking for holes. "Derek would have liked it."

She walks over to her desk, opens a drawer, and retrieves an envelope.

"He didn't have a card filled out; he wrote her a letter," Brooke says and passes it to me. "It's not sealed. You can read it."

"This is an invasion of privacy."

She shakes her head. "I helped him write it. Go ahead. I'm trying to show you that my shop is important to the community, and this is part of it."

I pull the letter out, lean my hips against the table, and begin to read silently.

My dearest Shelly,

If you're reading this letter, it's because Brooke has come to our home with a bouquet of flowers for you, after I've passed on. I'm so sorry, babe. I know you're having a hard time now, and I hope the flowers make you smile.

You've been amazing over the past two years since my diagnosis. You never left my side, spending every minute with me at the hospital, at the doctor's visits, and you saw things that no wife should have to see.

I don't know that I can ever thank you enough for your love. Being your husband was the greatest joy in my life, and I know that once I'm gone, I'll miss you every day. The way your hair hooks around your ear. The way you laugh when I tell my stupid jokes, and especially the way you sigh when I make love to you.

You are precious, and wonderful. You are the reason I held cancer back for as long as I did, because I wanted to eke out every moment I could with you.

I'm not going to get into boring things here. There's a will for that. This is to remind you how very loved you are. I will always be with you, and you will always be with me. I know we'll be together again, but take your time, Shell. Live your life to the fullest. Laugh and cry, sing and dance. Travel. And, when you're ready, marry again and have the babies we always longed for.

You have so much love in you. Don't keep it all to yourself.

I love you, babe. Forever.

XO, Derek

I fold the letter, blinking my stinging eyes, and return it to its envelope.

"Wow. He was young."

"Twenty-eight," she agrees with a nod, accepting the letter from me and tucking it in among the blooms. "His wife is a year younger."

"That's sad."

She nods again, lifts the bouquet, and says, "Let's go."

She secures the flowers in the back of her SUV and drives us the short distance to Shelly's house.

"This must be the hardest part of your job."

She considers for a moment, and then shrugs one shoulder. "Yes and no. I liked Derek, and I was heartbroken when he passed away. But delivering flowers like this is actually beautiful. I get to help comfort people during a time of great sorrow. It may seem like something small, but when they see the flowers, they have a moment of happiness, and that's important."

I reach over to take her hand and give it a squeeze.

"I agree. It's important."

Her brown eyes fly to mine in surprise as she parks the car and takes a deep breath.

"Here we go," she says softly.

We ring the bell, and the door is answered quickly.

"Hi, Blake," Brooke says, reaching her arm out for a hug. The younger woman smiles sadly, her eyes on the flowers.

"She's in the kitchen," she says, then looks at me. "Hi."

"Hi. I'm Brody. I'm just helping Brooke today."

She nods as she steps back, gesturing for us to come inside. "Nice to meet you. My sister will love these flowers." Her eyes find Brooke's. "Are these the ones?"

"They are."

"Oh man. I didn't think I could cry anymore, but it turns out I was wrong." She reaches for a tissue and leads us through the house to the kitchen. There are already dozens of bouquets of flowers set about, ranging from small to big, and all different kinds of flowers.

And when we reach the kitchen, a tall woman, probably five foot eight, with long blond hair, is standing at the island, dunking a tea bag in hot water.

"Hey, sweetheart," Brooke says as she approaches. She sets the flowers on the island, and Shelly's eyes fall to them. She looks tired. Maybe a little lost. And when she sees the sunflowers, her shoulders sag, whether in sadness or relief, I'm not sure.

"Oh, Derek," she whispers, and pulls the letter out of the blooms. "He's left me letters all over the place."

"That's sweet," Brooke says. "I'm very sorry for your loss, Shelly."

The other woman nods, a small smile touching her lips as she brushes her fingertips over the sunflowers.

"These were his favorite." She takes a deep, ragged breath. "But you already knew that."

"Are you going to read the letter?" Blake asks her sister. Shelly hugs the envelope to her chest and shakes her head.

"I've been saving them for bedtime because that's the worst time for me. It makes me feel like he's there with me."

"He is," Blake says and wraps her arm around Shelly's shoulders, giving her a supportive hug. "He's still here."

Shelly nods and smiles at Brooke. "Thanks for these. I'm sure Derek was in cahoots with you for a while. That's just how he was. A planner."

"I thought *I* was a planner, and I don't have anything on him," Brooke says with a small laugh. "We'd been planning this for about a year."

"A year," Shelly whispers. "That's when we thought he was in remission. He was feeling so good."

"And took the opportunity to get things in order, just in case," Blake adds, smoothing her sister's hair back from her face.

"Thank you," Shelly says to Brooke, holding her hand out to squeeze Brooke's. "This is really special."

"You're welcome."

After we've paid our respects, we're back in Brooke's car, headed back to the shop.

"I don't really know what to say." My voice fills the car, sounding louder than I intended. "I don't think I could do your job."

"There are sad days like today," she agrees. "But like I said earlier, it gave Shelly a moment of happiness. And, thankfully, not every day is like this. Just wait until Saturday."

"What's happening on Saturday?"

"You'll see."

Chapter Five

~Brooke~

It was a shit-tastic day.

I didn't let Brody see how horrible it felt to deliver those flowers to Shelly today. It was tearing my heart out of my chest. But I can't let the customer see that, and I need Brody to realize just how special my business is, and how the community needs it.

On top of being sad, it's a scorcher today. It's been a hot summer, hotter than normal, and for the first time since I bought my house, I'm regretting not having air conditioning added.

This house was built in the sixties. It's been updated, but no one ever added the convenience of A/C, mostly because we typically only have a few weeks of unbearably hot weather a year, so it really isn't worth the expense unless you're building a brand new house.

Not to mention, it still cools way down at night, and those of us who grew up here have mastered the art of trapping the cool air inside for the majority of the day.

This year, however, has been a Mother Nature shitshow.

I have several fans oscillating in each room, all of the doors and windows open, and I'm still a sweaty mess.

It's not dripping off of me, but I'm shiny for sure.

I'm in tiny shorts and a tank top. I can't make my clothes any smaller, unless I get naked. And right now, that doesn't sound half bad.

Just as I've decided to go take a dip in the lake, there's a knock on the front door.

"Hello?" Brody calls through the screen.

"Hey." I hold it open, gesturing for him to come inside. "Enter at your own risk. I'm living inside an oven."

"Is your air conditioning broken?" he asks, but my eyes are on the cold beer and pizza in his hands.

"No, I don't have it. Are we having a party?"

"The game's on," he says with a grin. "It's been a while since we watched the Cubs together, so I grabbed some game food and came right over."

I feel the smile slip over my lips. He thought to come here to watch the game with me.

Brody always was the sweetest guy I knew. Seems that hasn't changed.

"Fun," I reply. "I'll grab some plates. We should sit on the floor."

"Why?"

"It's cooler down there."

He blinks at me, considering, and then shrugs one shoulder and sets the pizza in the middle of the floor, sits, and opens the box.

"Thin crust pepperoni," he says. "I hope this is still your favorite."

"It is. I'll be right back." I hurry into the kitchen to get the plates, and take a moment to lean on the countertop, my hand over my chest, to catch my breath. If he keeps this up, I'll fall in love with him, and that can only lead to disaster.

He's leaving.

"The Cubs are winning," he calls from the other room. I grab our plates and join him, sitting a few feet away, and reach for a slice of pizza.

"O'Shaughnessy has been badass this year."

"He's badass every year," I reply around a bite of food, and then laugh when he frowns at me. "What? It's true."

"Hmm." He swigs his beer, and we fall into a comfortable silence, eating and watching baseball. "Oh, come on! You should have caught that!"

"You always did get riled up watching baseball."

He smiles at me, then wipes his mouth with a napkin. "There's no other way to watch it. God, you weren't kidding. It's damn hot in here."

"I know, I'm sorry. We could go somewhere else to watch the game."

"No, I like having you to myself," he replies, surprising me. "I'll just take my shirt off."

Before I can find enough brain cells to form a sentence, he whips his shirt over his head and tosses it onto the couch.

Jesus, Mary, and Joseph. Times a million.

I blink rapidly, trying not to stare at the tanned, toned, muscley goodness that is Brody Chabot, but it's impossible.

He's like the most glorious work of art in the world, and I'd challenge anyone to be able to look away.

His arms, his abs, his freaking *shoulders*, flex as he moves to grab another slice of pizza. How he can eat while all of my synapses are exploding one by one is beyond me.

I think I just lost all bodily function.

And I haven't even seen him all the way naked. This is just the upper half.

I bite my lip and take a sip of my beer, trying to distract myself.

If I thought it was hot in here before, it's officially lava-level now that Brody's taken off his shirt.

And I'm a puddle of melted goo.

The Cubs hit a homerun, and Brody thrusts his fists in the air, whooping in happiness. I smile at him, and then roll my tank top up my stomach and tuck it into the band of my bra.

"Sorry," I mumble. "Boob sweat is a thing, and it's damn uncomfortable." I sigh as my shirt soaks up some of the moisture and relieves me from the horrible stickiness.

But I come up short when I glance at Brody and find him with his beer halfway to his lips, and his eyes pinned to my flat stomach.

Interesting. I'm not the only one attracted.

Thank God.

No, this is bad. Bad! He's leaving soon.

However, my body gives zero shits about Brody's travel plans as his eyes rake up and down my scantily-clad body, and he swallows hard.

"Fuck," he whispers, setting his beer and plate aside. He moves over to me, unapologetically crawling over me, until I have no option but to lie flat on my back and stare up at him, both of us breathing hard, heat coming off of us in waves, and it has nothing to do with the temperature outside. "I've been keeping my hands off of you for days, when all I want to do is touch you."

"I'm not saying no," I reply softly, reaching up to brush my fingertips over his mouth. He pokes his tongue out, wetting his lips and my fingers, and the next thing I know, he lowers his face to mine and slides that mouth over my lips, starting slow and then sinking right into me.

Oh my God. I was right. He's an Olympic-level kisser. His lips are sure and skilled, sliding back and forth. He uses his tongue sparingly, just teasing me with it rather than jamming it down my throat.

That is the only point of contact between us, and I yearn for more. I want to feel the weight of him on me. I *need* to feel his skin.

With one hand on his forearm by my head, I glide my other palm down his toned back and slip it between his shorts and ass, squeezing in delight.

Holy hell, he's just hard *everywhere.*

And when he leans his hips in to rest in the cradle of my thighs, I notice that that's not all that's hard.

I moan against his mouth as he moves one hand down my sternum to my belly, pressing on my bare skin.

I want Brody Chabot more than I've ever wanted anyone in my life.

"My God, you'd tempt a saint," he whispers as his talented mouth moves along my jawline to my neck. He nibbles the sensitive skin there, giving me system-wide goose bumps. "And I've never claimed to be a saint."

"Good."

I feel him grin against me and his fingers slip lower on my belly, headed under my shorts to the promised land just as there's a knock on my front door.

We both freeze, our eyes pinned to each other.

"Ignore it," I whisper. "They'll go away."

"Your door is open," he whispers back.

"Doesn't matter. They'll go away."

"Oh for God's sake," Maisey says loudly. "Every damn window and door is open, Brooke. I can hear you. Now open this damn door."

I sigh, but neither of us moves for a moment. Brody brushes his nose against mine and then grins.

"To be continued."

I smile at his promise, and then we both roll away from each other, right our clothes, and I stand to head to the door.

"What do you want?" I ask.

"I'm excited to see you, too," she says with a laugh as I unlatch the door and open it for her. She's carrying a white pastry box. "Hey, Brody. I'm glad you're here. I need both of your opinions."

She doesn't even bat an eye at the fact that she just interrupted us rolling around on the floor together. It's as if she doesn't care in the least, or she walks in on things like this all the time.

Neither of those is true, and I know I'll get the third degree later. But I could kiss her for being so nonchalant about it.

Because I'm chalant as hell right now.

Maisey marches right past the pizza mess on the floor into the kitchen and lays the box on the table.

"I just came up with two new recipes, and I need to know what you think before I start offering them to customers."

"I'm your guy," Brody says with a grin and winks at me over Maisey's head. He put his T-shirt back on, but I can still see his naked torso in my head, and it makes me more than hot and bothered.

I was already hot.

Now I'm bothered.

In a really, really good way.

"Brooke," Maisey says, bringing me out of my lust-filled haze.

"Sorry, what?"

She smiles softly and holds a cupcake in her palm. "Here's the peaches and cream cake with whipped frosting."

"Fucking delicious," Brody says, already going back for a second one.

Maisey and I laugh as I peel the paper off of my cupcake and take a bite. I sigh in happiness, and take another bite. Then another.

"Jesus, Maise," I say, licking my lips. Brody has stilled across from me, watching my mouth as I enjoy the cake. "This is damn good."

"Yay, that's a yes. Now, try the white chocolate raspberry with vanilla ganache."

"Wow," I say as I chew the first bite. "The raspberry is really good."

"But is it as good as the peaches?"

I frown, take another bite, and look to Brody for his opinion. He shoves the whole thing in his mouth and reaches for another.

"I need to eat more to decide," he says, smacking his lips around the cake. I know he doesn't normally eat like this, thank God. He's just in cake rapture, and I totally get it.

Maisey can bake the hell out of a cake.

After we each eat one more of each flavor, we decide peaches and cream is our favorite, but that they're both winners.

"Excellent," Maisey says as she cleans up the cupcake mess. "Thanks, guys."

"I can't imagine that you've ever had a flop," Brody says, wiping his mouth.

"Oh, she has," I reply with a laugh. "Remember when you tried to make jalapeño cupcakes for Cinco de Mayo?"

"Yeah." She scrunches up her nose. "Ew. They weren't a hit."

"Okay, that doesn't sound fantastic."

"I also once tried to do a salted caramel that I just couldn't get right. I think I used the wrong kind of caramel."

"You should try that one again," I add as I reach for a sponge and wipe the crumbs off my table. "I bet you could tweak it and it would be awesome."

"Maybe," she says with a shrug. "I'm going to add these two to my fall lineup for brides."

"They'll be a hit," I assure her. "Are you ready for Saturday?"

She grins brightly. "Oh yeah. It's going to be fun."

Maisey and I love weddings. We have since we were kids, and I can't wait to see how it all shapes up.

"Okay, guys, I'm out of here. Go back to whatever it was you were doing. Just be safe."

She smirks and walks right out of my house. Brody and I stay in the kitchen, staring at each other until we hear her car start and she drives away.

And all of the doubts start to sink into my brain, now that it's functioning again. Maybe having Brody here for a whole week isn't such a great idea.

"I guess the moment is gone," he says softly, but reaches over to tuck a stray strand of hair behind my ear.

"Yeah." I clear my throat. "You know, Brody, you don't have to stay for the rest of the week."

He scowls, and I cringe, then pace away.

"I'm not saying this right. Well, I *am*, but I didn't mean to just blurt it out like that."

"You don't want me to stay?"

"I do." I bite my lip and turn, and he's looking all tall and gorgeous in my kitchen. "But I'm letting you know that if *you* don't want to stay, I'll be okay. I'll figure something out for the shop. You're not responsible for all of this anyway—"

"Stop talking," he says and crosses to me, wraps his arm around my low back, and pulls me to him. "I'm staying, Brooke. I don't know what this is exactly, but I feel it all the way to my bones, and I'm not willing to leave until we figure it out."

"Oh." I swallow hard, watching his mouth. "Okay."

"Are we on the same page?"

I nod, unable to say anything more when I'm pressed body-to-body with him. He brushes his lips to mine in a chaste, but still hot, kiss, and then backs away.

"I'll see you in the morning."

My fingers are still on my lips when I hear the screen door close behind him.

Chapter Six

~Brooke~

For the past three days, Brody and I have spent time together at the shop, delivered flowers, and stolen kisses here and there, whenever we found time alone.

Which, to my chagrin, hasn't been as much as I'd like.

He's had to spend time at the hotel in the evenings, working on his regular job, since I'm monopolizing so much of his days.

Part of me thinks I should feel a bit guilty for that, but I just can't bring myself to. I'm enjoying him, more than I expected.

Brody and I were friends when we were kids. We always got along well, and if I said I never had even a tiny crush on him, I'd be lying. But I was a young girl, and before I knew it, Brody stopped being my friend.

And then he was gone.

But I've quickly learned over the past few days that the young man I enjoyed so much is still there. Not only that, but he's grown into a sexy, kind, smart man, and it seems my body is more than a little hot for him.

I haven't felt tingles in my nether regions like this in, well, ever.

Brody Chabot is potent.

"How many of these are we doing?" Brody asks, pulling me out of my sexy reverie.

"Nine," I reply, then laugh at his look of shock. "This bride has nine bridesmaids. I already finished the bride's bouquet last night."

"You worked late?" he asks.

"Oh yeah, it was Thursday. I always work late into the night on Thursdays and Fridays in the summer. Saturdays are always booked up with weddings, and they take extra care and time."

"I offered to stay and help," Micah reminds me, his eyes pinned to the boutonniere that he's painstakingly putting together.

"You need rest too," I remind him. "Plus, you help me out a lot by spending all day on Fridays here."

"If I wasn't taking college classes this summer, I'd work full time," he says and then shrugs apologetically. "But you're the one who insisted I take the stupid classes."

"Because you're brilliant and that's what you *should* be doing," I reply, setting the finished bridesmaid bouquet aside and immediately starting the next. "I've thought about hiring weekend help."

"I have a friend who could use the work," Micah says, looking up at me now. "She's my age, she's smart and reliable. I can vouch for her."

"Have her drop in to talk to me," I suggest and smile at the sweet boy. Micah's been with me for a year and a half now, and frankly, I don't know what I'll do when he goes away to college.

"Cool. She needs the money. Her dad's a jerk."

I feel Brody stiffen beside me, but he doesn't say anything. Micah takes the box of finished boutonnieres to the cooler.

"You okay?" I ask Brody.

"Fine. Who chooses sweet peas for their wedding flowers?"

I laugh up at him. "That's what the bride wanted. They are a challenge, though, because they're fragile. Much more so than roses or peonies. But these should be fine for tomorrow."

"What happens after we do these?" he asks. He steps back, crosses his arms over his chest as he examines his handiwork, then returns to it, tweaking it just a bit.

My God, I want to climb him. He just fits here, tall and sexy, and frowning a bit as he concentrates on getting the bouquet exactly so.

I wonder if this is the look on his face when he's designing bridges.

"These will go in the cooler, and then we take the heartier flowers to the venue to decorate the space. The *whole* space. It'll be a late night for us, but I love it so much."

"I'm fine with that," he says with a grin. "Everyone's out of my office for the weekend, so I'm all yours."

All mine.

If only.

I admit that I don't just like Brody. I'm falling hard and fast, *very fast*, for him. I can't help it.

"Well, good, because I have plenty of work for you."

"Tell me what you love about weddings."

"What's not to love?" I ask with a chuckle. "Maisey and I have loved them since we were little, which is convenient, given the professions each of us chose."

"True. It would suck if you hated this."

"Exactly. I guess I love that it feels like a fresh start. A new chapter. I know it sounds trite, but it's true. Anything is possible after that day for these two people."

"And the wedding itself is an expression of them."

"You mean the bride," Brody says with a smirk. "Because I don't believe that men have much say."

"I disagree. You'd be shocked how many men have very specific ideas about what they would like to see at their wedding. Granted, some of them might get vetoed by their bride if it doesn't jibe with her vision, but they usually want to have a say."

"Interesting."

I nod. "So whether it's a big, lavish event like the one we're working on today, or something simple and intimate, I enjoy it."

We continue in silence for the next two hours, perfecting the last of the bouquets. Micah has moved on to the centerpieces. When we're all finished, I toss the moving truck keys to Micah, who runs out to drive it around to the front of my shop.

"We're not taking your car?" Brody asks.

"No, I rent a refrigerated truck for weddings," I reply. "I have too much to haul, and the flowers have to sit for a while as I move them. It's better if they're cold."

"You should buy a truck."

I laugh as Micah comes inside, ready to start loading the flowers.

"That's on my list of things, but I'm a small business, Brody."

He just nods, and the three of us work quickly to move the flowers in the summer heat to their cool reprieve in the truck.

Once everything is loaded, Micah drives the truck and Brody and I follow him in my car.

"You let him drive the moving truck?"

"He's a good kid," I reply. "He's been driving it for me for a year, and I've never had a problem. He's never been late for a shift, and he's never called out sick."

"Wow," he says in surprise. "That's more than I can say about some of my engineers."

"His work ethic is incredible, and he's a great kid."

He also needs this job so he can help support his mother because his dad is a piece of shit.

But I don't say that to Brody. That's not my story to tell.

I pull in behind the truck at the wedding venue. It's an old barn at the base of the mountain with a killer view of the lake and the nearby mountains.

If I ever get married, it'll be here.

I'm pleased to see the tables are set up inside the barn, already covered in linens, so we can set up centerpieces.

"Hey, Brooke," Dean Hernandez says with a wave.

"Hi, Dean." I smile brightly and offer the man a hug, then turn to introduce him to Brody. "This is—"

"Brody Chabot," Dean says with a grin, shaking Brody's hand. "Man, I haven't seen you in a long-ass time. How have you been, Brody?"

"Great, thanks. How about you? What are you doing out here?"

"I own this place," Dean says, holding his hands out at his sides and looking around. "I don't raise cattle, so I decided to make it an event space."

"It's the perfect place," I add with a grin. "And Dean's a dream to work with."

"I have the fridge cleared out for the flowers that'll go outside tomorrow," Dean says. "Feel free to load it up."

"I will, thanks."

Dean nods, then shakes Brody's hand again. "It sure was great to see you, Brody. I hope I'll be seeing you around."

Brody doesn't reply as Dean walks off, probably headed out to see to more wedding chores for tomorrow.

"Okay, Micah, go ahead and put as many of the outdoor flowers as you can in the fridge. It's air conditioned in here, so the centerpieces will be fine overnight."

With his marching orders, Micah takes off to get his work done, and I do the same. "Come on, Brody. This is going to be fun."

* * * *

"I don't remember the last time I was this exhausted," Brody says as he follows me into my house and collapses on the couch, staring at me with glassy eyes. "You do this *every* week?"

"You get used to it," I assure him.

"I won't," he says with a small smile. "And with all due respect, thank God for it because while I enjoy helping for a bit here and there, I don't think weddings are my thing."

"It's not for everyone," I reply and sit next to him. We're not touching, but the electricity has been humming between us all damn day. He would steal a touch here or there as he'd pass by me.

I'd send him coy smiles.

It's been a full day of foreplay.

And now we're both too exhausted to do anything about it.

Damn it.

I've thought of little else besides that kiss in this living room the other day. I'd like a repeat with far less clothing.

Our time is running out. Brody leaves Sunday.

And that just depresses me, so I push the thought aside, refusing to think about it.

"Your wheels are turning awfully fast for an exhausted person."

I chuckle and turn my head to look at him. His face is inches from mine. He smells earthy, from being outside most of the day.

Surprisingly, he doesn't smell *bad*.

Which he should because we also sweated our asses off in this summer heat.

But no, not Brody. He's too sexy to smell.

The thought makes me wrinkle my nose.

"See?" he asks, reaching up to smooth his thumb over my nose. "You're thinking hard."

"I need to stop thinking and go take a shower. I'm gross."

"Me too," he says with a sigh.

"You're not gross, and I'm not sure how you pulled that off."

"Trust me," he says. "I'm gross."

"I have two bathrooms," I offer. "You can use my guest bathroom if you want."

"Your hot water heater will support two of us in the shower at the same time?"

You could just come get in with me.

But instead, I just nod. "It's a new one. It should be fine."

Without giving it further thought, he stands and walks away, pulling his dirty shirt over his head. "Thank you."

Good lord, look at him go.

The back side of Brody isn't a hardship to watch in the least. Before I get myself all worked up into a tizzy, I walk into my own bathroom, start the shower, and shed my sticky, dirty clothes.

I turn the music on my phone on, as I always do when I'm in the shower, set the phone against the wall on the vanity, and then get under the cool spray of water, letting it wash away the grime from today.

Taylor Swift is shaking it off through my speakers as I push my head under the water and lather up my hair.

I have a lot of hair, but it's fine, so it'll dry quickly in this heat.

Once I'm rinsed and clean, I shut off the water and reach for a towel, but then realize that I washed towels yesterday and forgot to return them to the bathroom.

Crap.

Maybe Brody isn't out of the shower yet and I can just dart over to the dryer and get one.

I bite my lip as I open my bathroom door, walk through the bedroom, and poke my head out the door.

The coast is clear.

I hurry across the hardwood floor, leaving water droplets that I'll have to remember to soak up later. Just as I turn the corner to the laundry room, Brody walks out of the bathroom, covered only in a towel.

We both come to a screeching halt, and his gaze immediately falls over my body, setting me on fire all over again.

"Shit," I mutter and cover myself the best I can. "Sorry, I didn't have a towel."

He doesn't reply. He just rushes to me, lifts me in his arms, covers my mouth with his, and carries me directly to my bedroom.

Do not pass Go, do not collect $200.

"Fucking hell, do you know what you do to me?" he growls as he lowers me to the bed. His towel fell off somewhere in the hallway, and all I can see is Brody's body as he moves over me, each muscle flexing with his movements.

"Wow, you're sexy."

I feel my eyes go wide at the realization that I just said that out loud, but then I don't care when he plants one leg between mine, cups his hand over my left breast, and kisses me like he hasn't eaten in months and I'm an all-you-can-eat buffet.

Thank the baby Jesus.

He raises that knee and presses it against my core. I have no shame in grinding against him, moaning as my clit sends zings up my spine.

"You're so fucking sweet," he mutters, kissing down my neck to my collarbone. "I've done my best to stay away from you the past few days."

"What? Why?"

"Because I want to do *this*, and I didn't want you to think I was a forward asshole, but I just don't care right now, Brooke. I can't keep my hands to myself. Your body is what dreams are made of."

"No complaints," I assure him with a smile and dig my fingers into his wet hair, pulling him closer to me. "Touch me all you want as long as I get to return the favor."

"Tell me you have condoms."

I freeze, and then cuss under my breath. "I have an IUD, and haven't needed condoms in a *very* long time. They'd be expired by now."

His smile is instant and wolfish. "I'm clean. I promise."

I just smile and grind against him again, making us both sigh in delight. He plucks my nipple between his lips, then sinks in, sucking and biting the tender nub.

My hands are planted squarely on Brody's ass as he kiss up my neck to my mouth. He's hard, and I love the way his muscles flex as he moves.

Now, if only he'd shift between my thighs and sink inside me because I'm going *crazy*.

"God, you taste good," he says, working his way back down my chest to pay the other breast the same attention. "You've had me in knots, sweetheart."

"Same." I lick my lips. My hips officially have a mind of their own, circling and pulsing as he grinds against me, rubbing that smooth skin on mine.

He's not even inside me yet, and I feel like I'm going to explode into a thousand pieces.

"This first time might be fast," he warns me, his voice full of apology. "I'm sorry. We'll take our time later."

"Fast or slow, I don't care, as long as it's *now*."

He bites the skin above my breast and smiles up at me as he finally settles between my thighs. I move to put my legs up on his shoulders, but he shakes his head and untangles himself, easily moving into the traditional missionary position and framing my face in his hands.

"I want to see your face when I sink inside you the first time. Up close."

My breath hitches when he presses just the tip inside, waiting for me to adjust to him.

"You're beautiful."

"No, *you* are."

He smiles against my lips and pushes farther.

"Fuck me, Brooke, you feel so damn good."

"So good," I agree as he pushes the rest of the way, buried balls-deep inside of me.

"Are you okay?"

"Never been so good," I assure him, and smile when I flex around him and he cringes.

"If you keep that up, this will go faster than I thought."

I repeat the motion, and he swears again, then begins to move. It's slow and steady at first, but I cup his ass again, hitch my thighs a bit higher, and we both lose it.

He picks up the speed and I hang on for dear life as the orgasm builds, shooting through me and leaving me completely boneless.

Brody joins me, grunting my name, and then collapsing next to me.

"I'm going back for round two in just a couple of minutes," he warns me, making me laugh.

But we're both exhausted, and within seconds, Brody is snoring next to me. I kiss his cheek, then ease out of bed to clean myself up, turn the music off on my phone, and curl up next to him.

With my head on his chest, I fall into the deepest sleep of my life.

Chapter Seven

~Brody~

"Come on, sleepy head."

Someone pokes a finger into my cheek and then laughs when I brush it away. I'm hungover. I must have had too much to drink last night because my mouth is full of cotton and I have a splitting headache.

And who the fuck is the woman? I don't bring women home.

Ever.

"Brody, we really have to go soon."

I crack an eye open, and everything comes back to me. I'm in Montana, in Brooke's bedroom, and I had the best sex of my thirty years last night.

"Come here." I crook a finger at her, but she just grins and shakes her head no.

"There's no time to play," she says, and I notice that she's fully dressed in a flowy pink top, short black jeans, and her hair has been teased into a smooth twist at the back of her head.

She looks breezy and professional.

And she'd look better naked, with my hands fisted in her hair.

"I promised you round two," I mutter.

"And I'll have to collect later because we have a full day ahead of us and I'm already late."

I frown and reach for my phone to check the time.

"Jesus, it's nine."

"You were really tired."

I sit up, rub my hands over my face, and smile when Brooke offers me a steaming mug of coffee.

"Bless you."

"Drink it fast," she says with a laugh. "I need to get back over to the wedding this morning to give the bride her bouquet and make sure everything is perfect. Then, Maisey will show up to set up the cake, and I always help her. Cake is heavy."

"It's not an evening wedding?"

Brooke shakes her head no and then shrugs. "Like I said yesterday, thank goodness the barn is air conditioned."

"I've never heard of an air conditioned barn."

"Dean had it installed when he decided to remodel the barn and make it an event space. That A/C was worth every penny, especially with hot summers. So, the ceremony is outside, but the reception is inside. The ceremony begins at one, so we need to get a move on."

"Okay," I reply and try to clear my head. Apparently sweaty work and amazing sex leads to hangover-like symptoms the next day.

Who knew?

"I need food," I say and take a sip of my coffee. I already feel five percent better as I eye her over the rim. She's a little flushed from the early morning heat, and her eyes are happy as she watches me.

They flick down to my arms, then back up to my face.

I set my mug aside, then yank her to me, pinning her under me on her bed.

"Brody, my hair was done!"

"I give less than one fuck," I reply as I bury my face in her neck and nibble her there, careful not to leave marks. "You're too damn sexy for your own good."

"We don't have time for sex *and* food."

"Sex it is, then."

* * * *

"Oh, Brooke." The bride's eyes fill with tears as she takes her bouquet. "This is just *so pretty.*"

"Don't cry, Kelly," Brooke says, reaching in her pocket for a tissue. "Your makeup is perfect, and we can't have it running down your face."

"I've cried six times today," she sniffs and then shakes her head and tries to laugh it off, blinking her eyes furiously. "Okay, I'm not crying. Thank you so much. Everything looks beautiful."

"It's going to be a gorgeous day," Brooke promises her. "Micah's bringing in the bridesmaids' bouquets now. I'm going to head out to double and triple check everything and to help Maisey with your cake."

"Oh, I can't wait to see the cake," Kelly says, getting excited.

"I can't wait to taste the cake," a bridesmaid chimes in, making us all laugh.

"You're in for a treat," Brooke replies and gives Kelly a careful hug. "Now, relax for a bit, and enjoy your day."

"Thank you, Brooke. Really."

"You're welcome." Brooke winks and then leads me back into the barn from the small house reserved for brides that shares the property. "It's already so damn hot."

"Here's hoping the ceremony is a quick one," I agree. "Do we stay for that?"

"No," Brooke says. "We're almost done. Once we help Maisey with the cake and I just make sure the flowers look perfect, we jet out of here. It'll look like the flower fairies did their job."

"You're pretty incredible. You know that, right?"

She smiles, glances down, and her cheeks redden. She's so fucking sweet. It's no wonder that I've fallen for her this week. I've never known anyone like her, before or since she was in my life when we were kids.

We make our rounds of the tables, checking bouquets. She runs outside to take a look at Micah's handiwork on the outdoor arrangements. And just when she's finished, Maisey arrives with the cake.

I'm surprised to see that it's in several boxes, laying flat in the very back of Maisey's SUV.

"We have to move fast," Maisey says. "This heat will make the cakes sweat, and that's not pretty for photos. Be careful."

"Jesus, they're heavy." I take the biggest tier and hurry inside the barn to the far corner where the cake table is set up. The two women are behind me, carrying the last two tiers.

Maisey works like a woman possessed, opening the boxes and getting the cake assembled perfectly.

"Do you have my flowers?" she asks Brooke.

"Yep, they're in the fridge. I'll be right back."

Brooke sprints away, and as Maisey puts the finishing touches on the cake, she glances up at me. "How are you doing?"

"I'm great."

She frowns, and glances to the doorway Brooke disappeared through, then lowers her voice. "I know you and my sister have something going on. I'm not stupid. I also think it's pretty great, as long as you're not a complete dick about it."

I'm not exactly sure what to say, so I shove my hands in my pockets and frown at the woman who resembles her sister so closely. "Okay."

"Do you plan to be a dick?"

"No, I can't say that I do."

"Good. See that you don't."

Brooke hurries back with a small bouquet of flowers that match the bride's bouquet, and the two arrange the blooms on the cake. It looks random, but I know every placement is strategic.

"Our work here is done," Maisey says with a proud smile. "It's seriously gorgeous in here."

"I know." Brooke looks around, takes a deep breath, and I know in this very minute exactly what I'm going to do with my building.

"Do you want to take photos for your portfolios?" I ask.

"No, we'll get professional photos from the photographer," Brooke replies. "But thanks for thinking of it."

"I'm not selling," I announce, and two pairs of brown eyes fly to my face in shock.

"Really?" Brooke asks, practically jumping up and down.

"Really. Look, you've done what you set out to do. Brooke's Blooms is essential to this community, and with Maisey taking the space next door, you can expand both of your operations. Besides, the building is a good investment. We both win."

"I thought you wanted to cut all ties to Cunningham Falls," Maisey says.

"I've reconsidered."

They look at each other, high five, and then Maisey surprises the hell out of me by rushing at me, wrapping her arms around my neck, and laying a big, smacking kiss on my cheek.

Brooke follows suit, but her kiss lands square on my lips.

As if she remembers where we are, she pulls away, smooths her hands down her shirt and then walks toward the doors. Micah's waiting for us. "You can head out. You did a great job, Micah. Thank you."

"No problem. See you Monday."

He hops in the refrigerated truck and drives away, as the rest of us head out as well.

"I have one more stop," Brooke informs me. "And then, you're off the hook. You survived a whole week of designing and delivering flowers."

"It was actually really fun," I reply and reach over to twist a strand of hair that escaped around my finger. "I had a great week."

"I'm glad." She grins over at me. "I had a great week, too. I'm going to drop by my house first to change these clothes."

"Sounds good."

It only takes her a few moments to run inside and change into a tank top and a pair of shorts, immediately igniting my imagination and waking my cock from its lazy, post coital slumber.

"Great," she says when she jumps back in the car. "This is *much* better."

"Agreed."

She laughs, puts the car into gear, and drives us across town to a large house. There are several cars parked out front, with a play area for kids along the side. We climb out of the car, and she retrieves a bouquet from the back of her SUV.

She stops in front of me and bites her lip. "You know, you may not be able to go inside."

"Why?"

"This is a safe house for women and children who need a place to stay after escaping abusive situations, and they frown on male visitors."

My face stays passive, but I suddenly feel like I have lead in my stomach. Why wasn't this here when I was a kid?

Would my mother have come here with me?

"I'll be fine here," I assure her. Brooke rewards me with a bright smile and jogs up the steps to the front door.

Just after she disappears, another car pulls up next to Brooke's, and Micah climbs out, frowning when he sees me.

"Hey," he says. "What are you doing?"

"Waiting for Brooke. She had a delivery." I narrow my eyes as he takes a deep breath, looking up and down the street. "What are *you* doing?"

He pushes his hand through his hair. "I, uh, live here. With my mom."

What?

"I see. I had no idea, Micah."

"Well, it's not like I wear it on my sleeve that I have a piece of shit dad who likes to use us as a punching bag," he says. "There's no reason that you'd know."

"You're right."

He's completely right.

"Anyway, I should go in and make sure Mom's okay. Thanks for your help with the wedding."

"I had fun. Have a good weekend."

Micah waves and disappears inside, and I feel like I've just been kicked in the fucking face.

Of course I wouldn't know that Micah came from an abusive family, any more than anyone in this town would have known that *I* came from the same thing.

Because I didn't speak up. I was scared and embarrassed, and I kept it to myself.

They couldn't read my mind. They didn't protect me because they didn't *know* that I needed protecting.

Jesus, why has it taken me all of these years to figure this out?

"Ready!" Brooke announces as she bounces down the stairs to join me at her car. "Sorry for leaving you out in the heat."

"I understand," I reply, swallowing the bile in my throat. "I saw Micah."

She frowns and sighs deeply. "Yeah. He and his mom, Judy, have been living there for almost a year."

"You knew?"

"Of course." She frowns over at me before looking back to the road. "He works for me, and he would cringe when he carried the flowers into the cooler. His ribs were bruised. The fucker liked to kick him where he knew the bruises wouldn't show."

Fuck.

"So, I talked Judy into taking Micah there, and they've been thriving. She's filed for divorce, and her soon-to-be ex moved to Idaho for a job."

"But they're still living in the safe house?"

"Yeah, because Judy is disabled and Micah is working his ass off, but it's not enough to support them both. Thankfully, there's been plenty of space for them there."

I clear my throat, and then run my hand through my hair.

"What's wrong?" Brooke asks. She passes her house and keeps driving, and I'm glad. I don't want this shit to purge out of me in her home.

"I know how Micah feels," I say and hold my breath as she chews this information over in her head.

"In what way?"

"Glen used to beat the holy hell out of me."

She gasps and pulls over next to a park, currently empty, and gets out of the car, walking quickly to the swings that are under the shade of a giant maple tree.

I follow her, sit in the swing next to hers, and expect to see pity in her eyes when I look at her, but I just see anger.

"Whoa, are you mad?"

"No, I'm fucking pissed," she says, then takes a long, deep breath. "How long did he hurt you?"

"Three years."

"And you never said anything."

I shake my head, digging the toe of my shoe in the dirt under the swing.

"You just decided to stop being my friend. Why did you do that?"

"Because I was embarrassed. Hell, I'm still embarrassed."

"You were a *child*, Brody. And he was a grown man. There was nothing for you to be embarrassed about."

"I see that now, trust me. At the time, Glen was hot shit in this town, and I was just a kid. And trust me, I know I was stupid. I thought someone would read my mind and magically help me."

"Oh, my God." She digs her fingers into her eye sockets. "All that time, and I thought you just hated me."

"No, I was worried that you'd think badly of me when you found out that Glen used to enjoy kicking me in the gut until I coughed up blood."

She shakes her head, watching me with incredulous eyes. "My God, Brody. I'm so sorry."

"It's not your fault. Or anyone else's. Mom tried to stop him, but he would just do the same to her."

"Fuck, all that time everyone thought he was such a great man. The whole town mourned him when he died."

"I didn't," I admit. "I fucking danced. And what does that say about me?"

"It says that the man who terrorized you could no longer hurt you."

I take a ragged breath and nod. "Yeah. I offered so many times to take Mom away over the years before she died. She always refused. Always so damn loyal to him."

"Maybe she was afraid too, and not strong enough to be as brave as you were."

"Brave?" I scoff and then flat-out laugh. "Right. I fucking ran away."

"Exactly. And she never could."

I think about that for a long moment, then take another breath and look over at the most beautiful woman in the world. It feels like the world has been lifted off my shoulders. "I feel better. I'm glad we talked."

"Good." She stands out of her swing, and climbs on my lap, wrapping her arms around my neck and planting her gorgeous, plump lips on mine. She kisses me until my dick is at full mast.

"We're in public," I murmur against her lips.

"I'd take you to my place, but it's so hot in there that we'd die." She giggles against me, and my cock throbs.

"Let's go to the hotel. It's closer anyway. And I have a great view of the lake."

"Good idea."

She hurries to her car, and we drive the short distance to the hotel on the lake. Once we've given her car to the valet, and we're up in my room, she wanders around the space while biting her lip and checking out the view.

She suddenly seems nervous.

"What's up, sweetheart?"

"Nothing," she lies, kicking up a shoulder and avoiding my gaze.

"Look at me. What's going on in your gorgeous head?"

"Okay. I need to say this, just to make sure we're on the same page."

"Shoot."

"I am not having sex with you just to get you to keep the building."

And just like that, I see bright, flaming red.

"What the hell, Brooke?"

"I'm just saying—"

"Don't you *ever* insult yourself, or me, like that ever again. Me being in love with you has nothing at all to do with our business arrangement."

Chapter Eight

~Brooke~

I stare at him, blinking, certain that I've just heard him wrong.

"Um, what?"

He shoves his hand through his hair, in that way he does when he's especially frustrated, then props his hands on his hips and licks his lips.

"I said that out loud, didn't I?"

"You sure did." I cock a brow.

I love you too! God, I love him.

"You're not saying anything."

"Nope."

I want to giggle. I want to do a little dance, and then jump in his arms and let him make love to me until we're both a sweaty, exhausted heap of flesh.

But I really want to hear his words first.

"I do love you," he says, swallowing hard. "I thought that would be harder to say. I've never said it to anyone else, not since my mom."

I walk to him now and take his hand in mine, linking our fingers.

"You've surprised the hell out of me this week," he says.

"Same." I lean in to kiss his shoulder, and he presses his lips against my forehead, making me grin.

Forehead kisses from Brody are just the best.

"You're so damn smart, Brooke. And sweet. So fucking sweet."

He leads me to the bed and strips me bare, both physically and emotionally as he lists all of the many reasons that he's nuts about me.

I've never been more turned on in my life.

When I'm fully naked and writhing beneath him, he continues to pepper my skin with wet kisses.

"Brody."

"Yes, baby."

"You're making me crazy here."

He grins up at me. "That's my plan."

I smile, scissor my hips, and push against his chest, reversing our positions. I turn the tables on him, kissing his body, rubbing myself over him, and when he's groaning and moving uncontrollably, I rise up and lower myself over him, taking us both on the ride of our lives.

* * * *

"I love you too, you know," I murmur later when we're recovered and tucked under the covers, watching the boats skim over the lake through the large windows. "And this view."

"Whoa, don't change the subject." He tips my chin up so he can look me in the eyes. "Back up."

"I didn't want to say it when we were having sex because that just seems… I know, cliché. But I do love you, too. And I'm grateful that you inherited my building and came here to try to kick me out of it."

"I wasn't *kicking you out* exactly."

"I remember receiving a letter that said I had to leave."

"Okay, I was kicking you out."

I laugh and drag my fingers down his cheek. "But I need you to know that after this past week, even if you'd decided to sell, I still would have fallen in love with you."

"You would have been pissed."

I nod immediately, not denying it in the least. "Oh yeah. I would have been pissed. And heartbroken. But I would still be here."

"I don't ever want to break your heart," he replies, kissing my forehead again. "What do we want to do with the rest of our day? It's early yet."

"Hmm." I tap my lips and squint my eyes, like I'm thinking really, *really* hard. "Let's order room service and spend the rest of the day in bed."

"That's the best idea you've ever had."

* * * *

"Jesus, Ed makes the best damn pancakes in the world," Brody says the next morning. We're sitting in Ed's Diner, which is full to the brim with a few other locals and about a billion tourists.

It is summer in Cunningham Falls, after all.

"And the best omelets," I agree, taking a bite of my Denver omelet.

"It's damn loud in here."

I nod and glance around, a little sad that I don't recognize many of the customers. It's good for business because, although tourists don't usually buy many flowers, I have a whole shop filled with gifts and fun things to browse through and take home.

But the traffic suffers, and some of our sanity suffers along with it.

"It's amazing how the town has grown," Brody comments. "It seems to me that the infrastructure of the town wasn't built for this kind of growth in tourism."

"You're right," I reply. "If we'd come any later this morning, we never would have been able to park. Downtown is a nightmare in the summer."

"Is it worse in the winter, with ski season?"

"No, because a lot of the traffic is actually up on the mountain," I reply easily. "In the summer, people come for *all* outdoor activities, not just the mountain, although there is still a lot of interest up there for biking, hiking, zip lining, and a bunch of other things that the owner has done."

"Interesting," he says, nodding.

"What are you thinking?"

"I'm an engineer, so all of this is fascinating to me, that's all. There are ways to alleviate the congestion, but it's expensive."

"I like it when you start to use your professional terms," I say with a smile. "It's sexy."

He laughs, takes his last bite of pancake, and pushes his plate away.

"You're funny, Brooke." He reaches over to take my hand and gives it a little squeeze. "I'm going to miss you so much."

I blink at him, dumbfounded.

"What is it?" he asks.

"You're still *leaving* today?"

"Of course." He frowns, and I feel the earth fall out from under me. "I was always leaving today. You knew that."

"I thought—" I scowl and look down at the table, unable to finish the sentence.

So fucking stupid.

"Let's go." He signals for our waitress, pays the tab, and leads me out to the car. I drive us to my house where his car is waiting for him, quiet the whole way.

What is there to say? We just admitted to loving each other yesterday, and now he's leaving.

It sucks. And I don't know what this means for us.

When I pull into my driveway, I immediately get out of the car and march inside my house, opening windows and doors to get a cross breeze going.

This is the first time I can say that I hate my house. I should have installed the fucking air conditioning.

"Stop," Brody says softly. He's standing in the middle of my living room, his hands in his pockets, watching me with tormented eyes.

"What?"

"Stop this. You're running about here like mad, and you just look pissed off. We need to talk about this."

I feel my shoulders fall in defeat. "I don't mean to sound like a bitch here, Brody, but I'm not sure what there is to talk about. You're leaving, and I'm here. So, thanks? It was fun? Have a nice life?"

"Are you assuming that I'm never coming back?"

"No, you have a building here, so I guess you'll be back now and then."

"I'm coming back," he insists and pulls me to him, lowering his mouth to mine in one of his Olympic-style kisses. "I can't give you a timeline, but I *am* coming back."

"Okay."

"You don't believe me."

I sigh. "It's not that I don't believe you. I think you *want* to come back. But you have a job, and a life, and so do I. So, I just think it's going to be hard."

"I don't just have a job, I own the firm."

"You do?"

"Yes. So, I have some things to get in order, but it's not impossible."

"Owning the firm only complicates things," I argue, shaking my head.

"It's not forever," he promises, then checks his phone. "And I'd better go. I have to pack my things at the hotel and turn in my car before my flight in just over two hours."

I stare at him, and I want to *beg* him to extend his trip one more day. One more week.

But I can't do that. He's already done so much for me by staying this past week.

"I didn't realize you were leaving so early in the day."

Do not get needy, Brooke. No one likes that.

"I'm sorry, sweetheart." He kisses me once more, and I know this kiss is goodbye.

Whether it's goodbye for now, or goodbye for good, only time will tell.

"Be safe."

He smiles and frames my face. "I love you."

"I love you, too."

One more forehead kiss, and Brody is out the door. I don't watch as he pulls out of my driveway and away from my house.

Watching him go just seems like torture.

Last week, when I asked him to stay so I could prove a point, I had no idea that I'd be standing here, feeling like my whole world was about to implode. That I'd fall in love so completely and deeply, that for the first time in my life I would actually consider begging him to stay.

I'm not a begger.

And he's not here.

Chapter Nine

~Brody~

I haven't heard her voice in days. There just hasn't been time. I'm getting real tired of texts.

When I arrived in San Francisco, I came immediately to the office, and I haven't left since I got here. I've been working night and day to try to wrap this up and get back to Montana.

But as I stare at my team around the conference table, I'm beginning to lose hope that going to Montana will become a reality any time soon.

"Why didn't anyone contact me and fill me in on this while I was gone?" I demand. We lost a multi-million dollar client five days ago.

Five days.

"You weren't here," Brian Masters says with a shrug. "They were going to pull the plug with or without you."

"But probably less so if I'd had a fucking heads up so I could make some goddamn phone calls," I reply, and there's absolute stillness in the room.

I never lose my cool. Ever. It's my trademark.

Yet, here I am. Losing my cool.

"Brody—"

"I'm Mr. Chabot today," I interrupt. "Apparently you all need to be reminded who signs your goddamn paychecks. This is my company, and I don't care if I'm in Montana or Thailand, I can be back here in hours. I can be reached in seconds. Always. That hasn't changed."

I glare at every single one of them, even those who had no idea about Brian's fuck-up.

"Mr. Chabot," Brian says, his voice hard and his eyes full of resentment, "you were away on vacation, and this was a business decision that was easily dealt with without needing to consult you."

I stare at him for a long moment, rubbing my fingers over my lips. Brian's been at my firm since the beginning, but he's not a partner. He's a senior employee.

However, he's always enjoyed throwing his weight around.

"You're fired," I decide on the spot.

"What the fuck!" He stands, his hands in fists, outraged. "You can't fire me."

"Yes, I can," I reply.

"This company would be *nothing* without me."

"That's where you're wrong, and your biggest mistake. You actually believe that bullshit. You've brought a lot to this company over the past eight years, Brian, and I'm not excited to fire you, but you crossed a dangerous line, throwing away a lot of money with your ego. You're done here. Go pack up your office and leave quietly, or I'll call building security."

He glares, shoves his chair, and leaves the room without a word.

"He'll sue for wrongful termination," Jay, another of my senior employees, says.

"Let him try," I mutter and take a deep breath. "Now, we're going to get that client back, today. Jay, I want you on this one. You should have been from the beginning. Building this bridge in Tokyo is a big fucking deal, even if Brian would disagree."

We spend the next four hours poring over reports, plans, and ideas. By the time everyone goes to their offices, I lean back and rub my hand over my face in frustration.

My phone beeps in my pocket.

Just thinking about you. Love you.

I grin and type a quick reply. *Love you too. Call tonight. Promise.*

"You need to go home," Van says as he walks into the empty conference room. He drops into a chair across from me. "You're burning out."

"I'm busy. I was gone for a week."

He watches me impassively. "Go home," he repeats.

"I fired Brian."

"Oh, trust me, all of San Francisco knows. He hasn't been quiet about it."

"I don't care. I'm sick of him going over my head. Jesus, I *am* the head."

"Agreed."

"Did you know about this?"

Van's face doesn't move. "If I'd known, you would have known, too."

"We'll recover."

Van nods. "What do you need? Besides to go home?"

"I don't know." I drag my hand down my face for about the thirtieth time today. Van's right, I do need to go home, take a real shower, sleep for about four hours, and then get back to work. "I guess I'll go home."

"I had the kitchen stocked," he says and consults his phone. "You don't have any appointments until ten tomorrow morning."

"You did that on purpose."

He just blinks. Van's always been a stoic man.

"See you at nine, then."

"Excellent."

I return to my office to gather my suitcase and get some paperwork in order, but it seems Van already did that when I was in my meeting.

If I move to Montana, it would be best if Van moves too.

Jesus, I'm a prick. How can I expect my assistant to move to a different state, just because I'm in love?

That's demanding a bit much.

I shake my head and walk down to my car, which has a busted windshield, thanks to what looks like a baseball bat still sticking out of it.

I pull my phone out and call Van.

"Yes, sir."

"Call the cops. I'm not going home yet."

* * * *

"Jesus," I mutter in frustration. It's been a month since I left Montana, and it seems like I'll never be able to go back.

Not for any significant amount of time.

"I know you're trying to get to Montana," Van says, "but Mr. Tanaka only wants to talk to you."

"I can talk to him in Montana," I reply. "They have internet there."

"But the team is *here*," Van reminds me, watching me with cool gray eyes. He's still stoic, but I've worked with him long enough to know that he's frustrated with me.

"You think this is ridiculous."

"No, I don't. I think you're head over heels for this woman, and wanting to be with her is normal. But could she move here?"

"She has a business."

"So do you."

I shake my head. "Her business isn't easy to move."

"Neither is yours."

"Fuck." I take a sip of water, wishing it were something stronger. "So you're saying this is hopeless. That I should break it off so I can appease Tanaka?"

"I didn't say that," Van says.

"Stop being so fucking diplomatic and tell me what you *do* think."

"I don't know how you can have it both ways," he admits. "Don't deck me, but it's a tough situation. You make a *lot* of money, Brody."

"I don't give a shit about the money."

Van stares at me until I sigh, blowing out a deep breath.

"Okay, I care about the money, but it's not more important than her."

"What if you make this firm a partnership? That way, you can delegate more, and over time become more of a silent partner, commuting a couple of times a month."

I steeple my fingers, letting the suggestion roll around in my head.

It's a damn good one.

"What do you think about moving to Montana?" I ask him, and smile when his eyes widen in surprise. "I work better when you're around, and I would rather that didn't change."

"I've always wanted to see Montana."

"Do you like snow?"

He swallows hard. "I don't know."

"Well, if you're up for it, you may find out."

Before he can reply, my phone rings. It's Brooke, FaceTiming me.

"Hey, sweetheart."

"Hi." She smiles widely, then kisses the screen. "Thank you for these beautiful flowers. How did you manage to send me flowers without me knowing?"

"I called Micah," I reply. "He promised to keep it a secret."

"Well, he did a good job. Thank you."

"You're welcome."

She bites her lip. I'm staring at the screen, soaking her in. God, I miss her.

"Have you come any closer to having an idea on when you'll be able to come back?" she asks.

"Not yet," I reply, and watch as the hope dies from her gorgeous brown eyes. "I'm sorry, babe, I'm trying to get this all figured out."

"I know." Her voice is quieter now. "I'll stop asking you."

"You can ask all the time," I assure her. "Are we on for our phone date tonight?"

She nods and offers me a brave smile before we end the call.

"I have twenty fucking employees," I say to Van as I toss the phone down in frustration. "They don't need me to hold their hand. I like your idea of a partnership, and I'm going to talk to Jay right now."

"He'd be great at it," Van affirms, and I nod.

"It makes sense. Now, let's get this wrapped up so I can go home."

Chapter Ten

~Brooke~

The shop has been slow this week. With school starting, and the tourists leaving, the busy season is officially over.

And I'm totally okay with that. It was exhausting this year. Of course, it didn't help that as soon as Brody left, I completely saturated myself with work, staying at the shop late into the night and returning early the next morning, even when there was no need for me to be there that long.

I've never been so caught up on the bookkeeping and inventory since I opened my doors three years ago.

It's a beautiful day outside. Our unbearably hot summer turned into a gorgeous Indian summer, so I have the front door propped open with a brick, letting in the breeze.

"Go home," Maisey says as she breezes into my shop. She's been getting her new digs set up next door now that her busy wedding season is also finished. Once Brody decided to rent it to her, the process went incredibly fast.

"I could say the same to you," I reply as I open my laptop and wake it up. "When do I get to come and see what you've done over there?"

"When it's done," she says with a grin.

"You do realize that I can already see a lot of it from here."

"Stop peeking." She glares at me, then busts out into a dance. "It's so great, B. Also, I've decided on a name."

"Awesome, what is it?"

"Cake Nation." She giggles. "I know, it's not super romantic, but I want it to be neutral, to attract men and women. And I don't want people to think that it's just wedding cakes."

"I think it's a great name," I assure her and give her a tight hug. "I can't wait for you to get settled in, and then we can start to plan our joint events."

"It's going to *rock*," she agrees, then glances at the screen of my computer. "Why are you looking at real estate? That doesn't look like here."

I sigh and return to the computer, paging through listing after listing of storefronts. "It's in San Francisco."

She doesn't say anything, so I glance up to find her scowling and leaning on my countertop.

"What?"

"We just talked about joint events."

"I know."

"How are we supposed to have joint events if you've moved to San Francisco?"

"I don't know." I prop my head in my hands and rub my eyes until I see stars.

"You wanted *this* shop," she reminds me. Her voice is firm, but not unkind. "You asked Brody to stay so you could prove that *this* shop matters."

"I know that, too."

"If you were going to just leave and move to San Francisco, what was the point of any of that?"

"I don't want to move to California. Hell, I can't *afford* to move there," I reply and pace around the table. "I want to be here. I love my shop."

"I know you do," she says softly. "He's been gone a long time."

"Six weeks, two days, three hours," I reply and hate myself a little because I could break it down to the minutes if she asked me to. "And I don't think he's coming back, Maise."

"Well, you're wrong."

I jump at his voice and turn to find him leaning against the open doorjamb of my shop. I want to run over, jump on him, and kiss him until my lips are bruised.

"Hey, Brody," Maisey says.

"Maisey." He doesn't look away from me. His arms are crossed over his chest, his muscles bulging deliciously against his blue T-shirt.

He's better looking now than the day he walked out of my house.

"I'm just going to go back over to my new place," Maisey says, her voice nonchalant and breezy, but she stops in front of Brody and sticks her finger in his chest. "Don't be a dick."

She leaves and Brody comes inside, moves the brick, and closes the door behind him. We haven't taken our eyes off of each other yet.

It's like we're playing a super sexy version of chicken.

"Why didn't you believe that I was coming back?"

"Took you awhile," I reply when I can find my voice.

"That's not it," he says, slowly approaching me. "We've never lied to each other, Brooke. Let's not start now."

"Because you leave," I blurt out. "That's what you do. You left me before without a backwards glance, and I was starting to think that this time would be the same. That you'd get absorbed back into your life in California, and you'd—"

"What? Forget you?"

I nod, biting my lip to keep the tears at bay.

"I told you I was coming back. We've talked as often as possible since I left."

"I know." It's a whisper. "And I didn't think it was a lie."

"I had more to figure out than I anticipated," he replies. "And I'm feeling like the dick Maisey warned me not to be for keeping you waiting so long without any answers. I had to work some magic with my business in the city, to make sure that I can spend a significant amount of time away without jeopardizing the whole thing. I have twenty employees, and they would be devastated if I had to shut down."

"I had no idea." I wish he'd told me this weeks ago, then maybe I wouldn't have been so worried, so constantly disappointed. "You never said your business was that big."

"It wasn't a secret, we just never really talked about it."

"Because I was too busy worrying about keeping my own business open."

"Hey, that's okay. I had a great week with you. I just had to make sure that everything was under control so I could spend *many* weeks with you here."

"I don't think I can move to California."

He frowns. "I didn't ask you to."

"I know, but it might be easier for you. It's just, Brooke's Blooms is finally way in the black, and it took me a long time to get it there."

"I know that. I'm not suggesting you move to California with me."

"So did you come here to break it off?"

He stares at me for a long moment, then tips his head back and laughs.

Laughs.

"No, babe. I'm *here*. I have it figured out, and I'm here with you, if you still want me to be."

"Oh." That's all I can say as I blink at him, trying to soak his words in. "Really?"

He nods. "Can I touch you now? Because I wouldn't wish this kind of torture on my worst enemy."

I walk into his arms and hold on tight, relieved to finally have him home.

"You're staying with me," I mumble into his chest. "Don't rent a hotel room."

"I was hoping you'd say that." I can feel him smile against my hair, and the next thing I know, he boosts me up onto my work table, steps between my legs, and cups my face, then lays the kiss of all kisses on me, making me tingle *everywhere*.

"Missed you," I whisper against his mouth.

"Well, that's about enough of that."

Epilogue

One year later

~Brooke~

It's been a year since Brody walked through my door and my life changed.

I wiggle my ass in time with Rhianna as she sings through my speakers. I'm in the shop, and it's midnight, but I don't care.

I'm arranging my very own bridal bouquet. I've been fussing over it for two hours, adding roses, then taking them away again. I put greens in, then take them out.

I don't want too much green.

I'm marrying the man of my dreams tomorrow. We're supposed to spend tonight apart, according to tradition, and that means that I just can't sleep. It's hard to shut my brain down when Brody's not next to me.

I have no idea what he's up to this evening, and that's probably for the best. I trust him, and I know that he wouldn't do anything to embarrass us, or hurt me. I hope he's having fun.

I had dinner with Maisey and a few of my other friends, making it an early night. I want to be well rested, so my mind is sharp tomorrow.

The weatherman is calling for rain, but I defy Mother Nature to ruin my special day.

She wouldn't dare.

I've rented the beautiful barn from Dean, and everything is in place and ready for our evening event tomorrow.

Everything except this bouquet, because I just can't get it exactly the way I want it.

I've been mentally designing this since I was a kid. But I just can't make it look the way it does in my head.

"What are you doing here so late?"

I jump, covering my heart and dropping the flowers at the same time, which means I'll have to start over, and stare at my fiancé, who's leaning in the doorway.

I'm about to be his wife.

"I'm trying to get this bouquet right, but it's not coming together."

"I thought we were taking this week off?"

I smile at him as I gather the flowers again and start over. "We are. This is for my bouquet."

"Oh." He sighs, watching intently as I gather the blooms, then shakes his head. "No, I see the problem. You want this peony over here, by the rose. Not between the snapdragons."

I frown up at him. "Who's the floral designer here?"

"Hey, I learned from the best."

I smirk and shake my head, but when I really look at the flowers, he's right. That's exactly the problem.

I switch the flowers, and then laugh as he wraps his arm around my shoulders.

"You were right."

"Can I get that in writing? So I can show it to you over the next eighty years or so?"

I brush him aside and reach for the ribbon to tie it together. "You're a funny, sexy man. What are you doing here, anyway? I thought you were ogling strippers or something."

"Are there strippers in Montana?"

I stop to think about it. "Probably. Somewhere. Not here."

"Exactly. I was looking for you, but you weren't at the house."

"Couldn't sleep, and this needed to get finished. What's up? We're not supposed to sleep together tonight."

"Pity," he says, kissing my temple. "I wanted to tell you in person. You have thirty days to vacate the building."

I turn to him, frowning in confusion. "*This* building?"

"No." His lips twitch up into a smile. "Your house. I just heard from the builder today. We can move into our house any time. The A/C is ready for you."

"Oh my gosh, this is great news!" I hug Brody close and then let him sink into a toe-curling kiss. We started designing our dream house not long after Brody moved in with me last year. "Marriage *and* a brand new house, all in the same week. It's a lot to take in."

"All good things," he says.

"The best things," I agree. "You always seem to tempt me with the best things."

The End

* * * *

Also from 1001 Dark Nights and Kristen Proby, discover No Reservations, Easy With You, and Easy For Keeps.

Sign up for the 1001 Dark Nights Newsletter
and be entered to win a Tiffany Key necklace.

There's a contest every month!

Go to www.1001DarkNights.com to subscribe.

As a bonus, all subscribers will receive a free copy of
Discovery Bundle Three
Featuring stories by
Sidney Bristol, Darcy Burke, T. Gephart
Stacey Kennedy, Adriana Locke
JB Salsbury, and Erika Wilde

Discover 1001 Dark Nights Collection Five

Go to www.1001DarkNights.com for more information.

BLAZE ERUPTING by Rebecca Zanetti
Scorpius Syndrome/A Brigade Novella

ROUGH RIDE by Kristen Ashley
A Chaos Novella

HAWKYN by Larissa Ione
A Demonica Underworld Novella

RIDE DIRTY by Laura Kaye
A Raven Riders Novella

ROME'S CHANCE by Joanna Wylde
A Reapers MC Novella

THE MARRIAGE ARRANGEMENT by Jennifer Probst
A Marriage to a Billionaire Novella

SURRENDER by Elisabeth Naughton
A House of Sin Novella

INKED NIGHT by Carrie Ann Ryan
A Montgomery Ink Novella

ENVY by Rachel Van Dyken
An Eagle Elite Novella

PROTECTED by Lexi Blake
A Masters and Mercenaries Novella

THE PRINCE by Jennifer L. Armentrout
A Wicked Novella

PLEASE ME by J. Kenner
A Stark Ever After Novella

WOUND TIGHT by Lorelei James
A Rough Riders/Blacktop Cowboys Novella®

STRONG by Kylie Scott
A Stage Dive Novella

DRAGON NIGHT by Donna Grant
A Dark Kings Novella

TEMPTING BROOKE by Kristen Proby
A Big Sky Novella

HAUNTED BE THE HOLIDAYS by Heather Graham
A Krewe of Hunters Novella

CONTROL by K. Bromberg
An Everyday Heroes Novella

HUNKY HEARTBREAKER by Kendall Ryan
A Whiskey Kisses Novella

THE DARKEST CAPTIVE by Gena Showalter
A Lords of the Underworld Novella

Discover 1001 Dark Nights Collection One

Go to www.1001DarkNights.com for more information.

FOREVER WICKED by Shayla Black
CRIMSON TWILIGHT by Heather Graham
CAPTURED IN SURRENDER by Liliana Hart
SILENT BITE: A SCANGUARDS WEDDING by Tina Folsom
DUNGEON GAMES by Lexi Blake
AZAGOTH by Larissa Ione
NEED YOU NOW by Lisa Renee Jones
SHOW ME, BABY by Cherise Sinclair
ROPED IN by Lorelei James
TEMPTED BY MIDNIGHT by Lara Adrian
THE FLAME by Christopher Rice
CARESS OF DARKNESS by Julie Kenner

Also from 1001 Dark Nights

TAME ME by J. Kenner

Discover 1001 Dark Nights Collection Two

Go to www.1001DarkNights.com for more information.

WICKED WOLF by Carrie Ann Ryan
WHEN IRISH EYES ARE HAUNTING by Heather Graham
EASY WITH YOU by Kristen Proby
MASTER OF FREEDOM by Cherise Sinclair
CARESS OF PLEASURE by Julie Kenner
ADORED by Lexi Blake
HADES by Larissa Ione
RAVAGED by Elisabeth Naughton
DREAM OF YOU by Jennifer L. Armentrout
STRIPPED DOWN by Lorelei James
RAGE/KILLIAN by Alexandra Ivy/Laura Wright
DRAGON KING by Donna Grant
PURE WICKED by Shayla Black
HARD AS STEEL by Laura Kaye
STROKE OF MIDNIGHT by Lara Adrian
ALL HALLOWS EVE by Heather Graham
KISS THE FLAME by Christopher Rice
DARING HER LOVE by Melissa Foster
TEASED by Rebecca Zanetti
THE PROMISE OF SURRENDER by Liliana Hart

Also from 1001 Dark Nights

THE SURRENDER GATE By Christopher Rice
SERVICING THE TARGET By Cherise Sinclair

Discover 1001 Dark Nights Collection Three

Go to www.1001DarkNights.com for more information.

Discover 1001 Dark Nights Collection Four

Go to www.1001DarkNights.com for more information.

ROCK CHICK REAWAKENING by Kristen Ashley
ADORING INK by Carrie Ann Ryan
SWEET RIVALRY by K. Bromberg
SHADE'S LADY by Joanna Wylde
RAZR by Larissa Ione
ARRANGED by Lexi Blake
TANGLED by Rebecca Zanetti
HOLD ME by J. Kenner
SOMEHOW, SOME WAY by Jennifer Probst
TOO CLOSE TO CALL by Tessa Bailey
HUNTED by Elisabeth Naughton
EYES ON YOU by Laura Kaye
BLADE by Alexandra Ivy/Laura Wright
DRAGON BURN by Donna Grant
TRIPPED OUT by Lorelei James
STUD FINDER by Lauren Blakely
MIDNIGHT UNLEASHED by Lara Adrian
HALLOW BE THE HAUNT by Heather Graham
DIRTY FILTHY FIX by Laurelin Paige
THE BED MATE by Kendall Ryan
PRINCE ROMAN by CD Reiss
NO RESERVATIONS by Kristen Proby
DAWN OF SURRENDER by Liliana Hart

Also from 1001 Dark Nights

TEMPT ME by J. Kenner

About Kristen Proby

New York Times and *USA Today* bestselling author Kristen Proby has published more than thirty romance novels. She is best known for her self-published With Me In Seattle and Boudreaux series, and also works with William Morrow on the Fusion Series. Kristen lives in Montana with her husband, their pug and two cats.

Discover More Kristen Proby

No Reservations
A Fusion Novella
By Kristen Proby

New York Times Bestselling author Kristen Proby takes us back to her highly acclaimed Fusion series.

Chase MacKenzie is *not* the man for Maura Jenkins. A self-proclaimed life-long bachelor, and unapologetic about his distaste for monogamy, a woman would have to be a masochist to want to fall into Chase's bed.

And Maura is no masochist.

Chase has one strict rule: no strings attached. Which is fine with Maura because she doesn't even really *like* Chase. He's arrogant, cocky, and let's not forget bossy. But when he aims that crooked grin at her, she goes weak in the knees. Not that she has any intentions of falling for his charms.

Definitely not.

Well, maybe just once…

* * * *

Easy For Keeps
A Boudreaux Novella
By Kristen Proby

Adam Spencer loves women. All women. Every shape and size, regardless of hair or eye color, religion or race, he simply enjoys them all. Meeting more than his fair share as the manager and head bartender of The Odyssey, a hot spot in the heart of New Orleans' French Quarter, Adam's comfortable with his lifestyle, and sees no reason to change it. A wife and kids, plus the white picket fence are not in the cards for this confirmed bachelor. Until a beautiful woman, and her sweet princess, literally knock him on his ass.

Sarah Cox has just moved to New Orleans, having accepted a position as a social worker specializing in at-risk women and children. It's a demanding, sometimes dangerous job, but Sarah is no shy wallflower. She can handle just about anything that comes at her, even the attentions of one sexy Adam Spencer. Just because he's charmed her daughter, making her think of magical kingdoms with happily ever after, doesn't mean that Sarah believes in fairy tales. But the more time she spends with the enchanting man, the more he begins to sway her into believing in forever.

Even so, when Sarah's job becomes more dangerous than any of them bargained for, will she be ripped from Adam's life forever?

* * * *

Easy With You
A With You In Seattle Novella
By Kristen Proby

Nothing has ever come easy for Lila Bailey. She's fought for every good thing in her life during every day of her thirty-one years. Aside from that one night with an impossible to deny stranger a year ago, Lila is the epitome of responsible.

Steadfast. Strong.

She's pulled herself out of the train wreck of her childhood, proud to be a professor at Tulane University and laying down roots in a city she's grown to love. But when some of her female students are viciously murdered, Lila's shaken to the core and unsure of whom she can trust in New Orleans. When the police detective assigned to the murder case comes to investigate, she's even more surprised to find herself staring into the eyes of the man that made her toes curl last year.

In an attempt to move on from the tragic loss of his wife, Asher Smith moved his daughter and himself to a new city, ready for a fresh start. A damn fine police lieutenant, but new to the New Orleans force, Asher has a lot to prove to his colleagues and himself.

With a murderer terrorizing the Tulane University campus, Asher finds himself toe-to-toe with the one woman that haunts his dreams. His hands, his lips, his body know her as intimately as he's ever known anyone. As he learns her mind and heart as well, Asher wants nothing more than to keep her safe, in his bed, and in his and his daughter's lives for the long haul.

But when Lila becomes the target, can Asher save her in time, or will he lose another woman he loves?

Kristen Proby Crossover Collection

Everyone knows there's nothing I love more than a happy ending. It's what I do for a living–I'm in LOVE with love. And what's better than love? More love, of course!

Just imagine, Louis Vuitton and Tiffany, collaborating on the world's most perfect handbag. Jimmy Choo and Louboutin, making shoes just for me. Not loving enough? What if Hugh Grant in *Notting Hill* was the man to barge into Sandra Bullock's office in *The Proposal*? I think we can all agree that Julia Roberts' character would have had her hands full with Ryan Reynolds.

Now imagine what would happen if one of the characters from my Big Sky Series met up with other characters from some of your favorite authors from their series. Well, wonder no more because in March of 2019, The Kristen Proby Crossover Collection is coming your way, and I could not be more excited.

Rachel Van Dyken, Laura Kaye, Sawyer Bennett, Monica Murphy, Samantha Young, and K.L. Grayson are all bringing their own beloved characters to play – and find their happy endings – in my world. Can you imagine all the love, laughter and shenanigans in store?

Love,
Kristen Proby

Soaring with Fallon: A Big Sky Novel
By Kristen Proby

Fallon McCarthy has climbed the corporate ladder. She's had the office with the view, the staff, and the plaque on her door. The unexpected loss of her grandmother taught her that there's more to life than meetings and conference calls, so she quit, and is happy to be a nomad, checking off items on her bucket list as she takes jobs teaching yoga in each place she lands in. She's happy being free, and has no interest in being tied down.

When Noah King gets the call that an eagle has been injured, he's not expecting to find a beautiful stranger standing vigil when he arrives. Rehabilitating birds of prey is Noah's passion, it's what he lives for, and he doesn't have time for a nosy woman who's suddenly taken an interest in Spread Your Wings sanctuary.

But Fallon's gentle nature, and the way she makes him laugh, and *feel* again draws him in. When it comes time for Fallon to move on, will Noah's love be enough for her to stay, or will he have to find the strength to let her fly?

* * * *

Wicked Force: A Wicked Horse Vegas/Big Sky Novella
By Sawyer Bennett

From *New York Times* and *USA Today* bestselling author Sawyer Bennett…

Joslyn Meyers has taken the celebrity world by storm, drawing the attention of millions. But one fan's affections has gone too far, and she's running to the one place she hopes he'll never find her – back home to Cunningham Falls.

Kynan McGrath leads The Jameson Group, a world-class security organization, and he's ready to do what it takes to keep Joslyn safe, even if it means giving up his own life in return. The one thing he's not prepared to lose, though, is his heart.

* * * *

Crazy Imperfect Love: A Dirty Dicks/Big Sky Novella
By KL Grayson

From *USA Today* bestselling author KL Grayson...

Abigail Darwin needs one thing in life: consistency. Okay, make that two things: consistency and order. Tired of being shackled to her obsessive-compulsive mind, Abigail is determined to break free. Which is why she's shaking things up.

Fresh out of nursing school, she takes a traveling nurse position. A new job in a new city every few months? That's a sure-fire way to keep her from settling down and falling into old habits. First stop, Cunningham Falls, Montana.

The only problem? She didn't plan on falling in love with the quaint little town, and she sure as heck didn't plan on falling for its resident surgeon, Dr. Drake Merritt

Laid back, messy, and spontaneous, Drake is everything she's not. But he is completely smitten by the new, quirky nurse working on the med-surg floor of the hospital.

Abby puts up a good fight, but Drake is determined to break through her carefully erected walls to find out what makes her tick. And sigh and moan and smile and laugh. Because he really loves her laugh.

But falling in love isn't part of Abby's plan. Will Drake have what it takes to convince her that the best things in life come from doing what scares us the most?

* * * *

Worth Fighting For: A Warrior Fight Club/Big Sky Novella
By Laura Kaye

From *New York Times* and *USA Today* bestselling author Laura Kaye...

Getting in deep has never felt this good...

Commercial diving instructor Tara Hunter nearly lost everything in an accident that saw her medically discharged from the navy. With the help of the Warrior Fight Club, she's fought hard to overcome her fears and get back in the water where she's always felt most at home. At work, she's tough, serious, and doesn't tolerate distractions. Which is why finding her gorgeous one-night stand on her new dive team is such a problem.

Former navy deep-sea diver Jesse Anderson just can't seem to stop making mistakes—the latest being the hot-as-hell night he'd spent with his new partner. This job is his second chance, and Jesse knows he shouldn't mix business with pleasure. But spending every day with Tara's smart mouth and sexy curves makes her so damn hard to resist.

Joining a wounded warrior MMA training program seems like the perfect way to blow off steam—until Jesse finds that Tara belongs too. Now they're getting in deep and taking each other down day and night, and even though it breaks all the rules, their inescapable attraction might just be the only thing truly worth fighting for.

* * * *

Nothing Without You: A Forever Yours/Big Sky Novella
By Monica Murphy

From *New York Times* and *USA Today* bestselling author Monica Murphy...

Designing wedding cakes is Maisey Henderson's passion. She puts her heart and soul into every cake she makes, especially since she's such a believer in true love. But then Tucker McCloud rolls back into town, reminding her that love is a complete joke. The pro football player is the hottest thing to come out of Cunningham Falls—and the boy who broke Maisey's heart back in high school.

He claims he wants another chance. She says absolutely not. But Maisey's refusal is the ultimate challenge to Tucker. Life is a game, and Tucker's playing to win Maisey's heart—forever.

* * * *

All Stars Fall: A Seaside Pictures/Big Sky Novella
By Rachel Van Dyken

From *New York Times* and *USA Today* bestselling author Rachel Van Dyken...

She *left*.
Two words I can't really get out of my head.
She left *us*.
Three more words that make it that much worse.
Three being another word I can't seem to wrap my mind around.
Three kids under the age of six, and she left because she missed it. Because her dream had never been to have a family, no her dream had been to marry a rockstar and live the high life.

Moving my recording studio to Seaside Oregon seems like the best idea in the world right now especially since Seaside Oregon has turned into the place for celebrities to stay and raise families in between touring and producing. It would be lucrative to make the move, but I'm doing it for my kids because they need normal, they deserve normal. And me? Well, I just need a break and help, that too. I need a sitter and fast. Someone who won't flip me off when I ask them to sign an Iron Clad NDA, someone who won't sell our pictures to the press, and most of all? Someone who looks absolutely nothing like my ex-wife.

He's tall.

That was my first instinct when I saw the notorious Trevor Wood, drummer for the rock band Adrenaline, in the local coffee shop. He ordered a tall black coffee which made me smirk, and five minutes later I somehow agreed to interview for a nanny position. I couldn't help it; the smaller one had gum stuck in her hair while the eldest was standing on his feet and asking where babies came from. He looked so pathetic, so damn sexy and pathetic that rather than be star-struck, I took pity. I knew though; I knew the minute I signed that NDA, the minute our fingers brushed and my body became insanely aware of how close he was—I was in dangerous territory, I just didn't know how dangerous until it was too late. Until I fell for the star and realized that no matter how high they are in the sky—they're still human and fall just as hard.

* * * *

Hold On: A Play On/Big Sky Novella
By Samantha Young

From *New York Times* and *USA Today* bestselling author Samantha Young...

Autumn O'Dea has always tried to see the best in people while her big brother, Killian, has always tried to protect her from the worst. While their lonely upbringing made Killian a cynic, it isn't in Autumn's nature to be anything but warm and open. However, after a series of relationship disasters and the unsettling realization that she's drifting aimlessly through life, Autumn wonders if she's left herself too vulnerable to the world. Deciding some distance from the security blanket of her brother and an unmotivated life in Glasgow is exactly what she needs to find herself, Autumn takes up her friend's offer to stay at a ski resort in the snowy hills of Montana. Some guy-free alone time on Whitetail Mountain sounds just the thing to get to know herself better.

However, she wasn't counting on colliding into sexy Grayson King on the slopes. Autumn has never met anyone like Gray. Confident, smart, with a wicked sense of humor, he makes the men she dated seem like boys. Her attraction to him immediately puts her on the defense because being open-hearted in the past has only gotten it broken. Yet it becomes increasingly difficult to resist a man who is not only determined to seduce her, but adamant about helping her find her purpose in life and embrace the person she is. Autumn knows she shouldn't fall for Gray. It can only end badly. After all their lives are divided by an ocean and their inevitable separation is just another heart break away...

On behalf of 1001 Dark Nights,

Liz Berry and M.J. Rose would like to thank ~

Steve Berry
Doug Scofield
Kim Guidroz
Jillian Stein
InkSlinger PR
Dan Slater
Asha Hossain
Chris Graham
Fedora Chen
Kasi Alexander
Jessica Johns
Dylan Stockton
Richard Blake
and Simon Lipskar

Made in the USA
Columbia, SC
22 October 2018